LUNATICS, LOVERS & POETS

LUNATICS, LOVERS & POETS

*Twelve stories after
Cervantes and Shakespeare*

EDITED BY
Daniel Hahn & Margarita Valencia

LOS ANGELES · HIGH WYCOMBE

HAY FESTIVAL
AFRICA AMERICAS ASIA EUROPE MIDDLE EAST

First published by And Other Stories, 2016
High Wycombe, England – Los Angeles, USA
www.andotherstories.org

ISBN 9781908276780
eBook ISBN 9781908276797

A catalogue record for this book is available from the British Library.

Copy-editor: Ana Fletcher; Typesetter: Tetragon, London; Typefaces: Linotype Swift Neue, Verlag; Cover Design: Hannah Naughton. Printed and bound by the CPI Group (UK) Ltd, Croydon, CR0 4YY.

This project was undertaken with the generous support of the British Council and AC/E (Acción Cultural Española). And Other Stories is also supported by public funding from Arts Council England.

CONTENTS

INTRODUCTION

Salman Rushdie

As we honour the four hundredth anniversaries of the deaths of William Shakespeare and Miguel de Cervantes Saavedra, it may be worth noting that while it's generally accepted that the two giants died on the same date, 23 April 1616, it actually wasn't the same day. By 1616 Spain had moved on to using the Gregorian calendar, while England still used the Julian, and was eleven days behind. (England clung to the old Julian dating system until 1752, and when the change finally came, there were riots and, it's said, mobs in the streets shouting 'Give us back our eleven days!') Both the coincidence of the dates and the difference in the calendars would, one suspects, have delighted the playful, erudite sensibilities of the two fathers of modern literature.

We don't know if they were aware of each other, but they had a good deal in common, beginning right there in the 'don't know' zone, because they are both men of mystery, there are missing years in the record and, even more tellingly, missing documents. Neither man left behind much personal material. Very little to nothing in the way of letters, work diaries, abandoned drafts; just the colossal, completed oeuvres. 'The rest is silence.' Consequently, both men have been prey to the kind of idiot theories that seek to dispute their authorship. A cursory internet search 'reveals', for example, that not only did Francis Bacon write Shakespeare's works, *he wrote Don Quixote as well.* (My favourite crazy Shakespeare theory is that his plays were not written by him but by someone else of the same name.) And of course Cervantes faced a challenge to his authorship in his own lifetime, when a certain pseudonymous Alonso Fernández de Avellaneda, whose identity is also uncertain, published his fake sequel to *Don Quixote* and goaded Cervantes into writing the real Book Two, whose characters are aware of the plagiarist Avellaneda and hold him in much contempt.

Cervantes and Shakespeare almost certainly never met, but the closer you look at the pages they left behind the more echoes you hear. The first, and to my mind the most valuable shared idea is the belief that a work of literature doesn't have to be simply comic, or tragic, or romantic, or political / historical: that, if properly conceived, it can be many things at the same time.

Take a look at the opening scenes of *Hamlet.* Act One, Scene One is a ghost story. 'Is not this something more than fantasy?' Barnardo asks Horatio, and of course the play is much more than that. Act One, Scene Two brings on the intrigue at the court of Elsinore: the angry scholar prince, his recently widowed mother wedded to his uncle ('O most wicked speed / To post with such dexterity to incestuous sheets'). Act One, Scene Three, and here's Ophelia, telling her dubious father Polonius the beginning of what will become a sad love story: 'My lord, he hath importuned me with love / In honourable fashion.' Act One, Scene Four, and it's a ghost story again, and something is rotten in the state of Denmark. As the play proceeds, it goes on metamorphosing, becoming by turns a suicide story, a murder story, a political conspiracy and a revenge tragedy. It has comic moments and a play within the play. It contains some of the highest poetry ever written in English and it ends in melodramatic puddles of blood.

This is what we who come after inherit from the Bard: the knowledge a work can be everything at once. The French tradition, more severe, separates tragedy (Racine) and comedy (Molière). Shakespeare mashes them up together, and so, thanks to him, can we.

In a famous essay, Milan Kundera proposed that the novel has two progenitors, Samuel Richardson's *Clarissa* and Laurence Sterne's *Tristram Shandy*; yet both these voluminous, encyclopaedic fictions show the influence of Cervantes. Sterne's Uncle Toby and Corporal Trim are openly modelled on Quixote and Sancho Panza, while Richardson's realism owes a good deal to Cervantes's debunking of the foolish mediaeval literary tradition whose delusions hold Don Quixote in thrall.

In Cervantes's masterpiece, as in Shakespeare's work, pratfalls coexist with nobility, pathos and emotion with bawdiness and ribaldry, culminating in the infinitely moving moment when the real world asserts itself and the Knight of the Dolorous Countenance accepts that he has been a foolish, mad old man, 'looking for this year's birds in last year's nests.'

They are both self-conscious writers, modern in a way that most of the modern masters would recognise, the one creating plays that are highly aware of their theatricality, of being staged; the other creating fiction that is acutely conscious of its fictive nature, even to the point of inventing an imaginary narrator, Cide Hamete Benengeli – a narrator, interestingly, with Arab antecedents.

And they are both as fond of, and adept at, low life as they are of high ideas, and their galleries of rascals, whores, cutpurses and drunks would be at home in the same taverns. This earthiness is what reveals them both to be realists in the grand manner, even when they are posing as fantasists, and so, again, we who come after can learn from them that magic is pointless except when in the service of realism – was there ever a more realist magician than Prospero? – and realism can do with the injection of a healthy dose of the fabulist. Finally, though they both use tropes that originate in folktale, myth and fable, they refuse to moralise, and in this above all else they are more modern than many who followed them.

They do not tell us what to think or feel, but they show us how to do so.

Of the two, Cervantes was the man of action, fighting in battles, being seriously wounded, losing the use of his left hand, being enslaved by the corsairs of Algiers for five years until his family raised the money for his ransom. Shakespeare had no such dramas in his personal experience; yet of the two he seems to have been the writer more interested in war and soldiering. *Othello*, *Macbeth*, *Lear* are all tales of men at war (within themselves, yes, but on the field of battle, too). Cervantes used his painful experiences, for example in the Captive's Tale in *Quixote* and in a couple of plays, but the battle on which Don Quixote embarks is – to use modern words – absurdist and existential rather than 'real'. Strangely, the Spanish warrior wrote of the comic futility of going into battle and created the great iconic figure of the warrior as fool (one thinks of Heller's *Catch-22* or Vonnegut's *Slaughterhouse-Five* for more recent explorations of this theme), while the imagination of the English poet-dramatist plunged (like Tolstoy, like Mailer) headlong towards war.

In their differences, they embody very contemporary opposites, just as, in their similarities, they agree on a great deal that is still useful to their inheritors; of whom a very distinguished selection will have more to say in the pages that follow hereafter.

DON QUIXOTE AND THE AMBIGUITY OF READING

Ben Okri

When he came into the printing workshop, we thought he was drunk. He had come to see for himself the machine that multiplies realities. He came in with his machete drawn. He had been passing by on one of his adventures to the North. He had heard that there was a war going on between giants and men. He wanted to fight against the giants. He claimed to have fought them before.

When he came into the shop he had the idea that the printing machine was in some way antagonistic to him. We had been working the shafts and the steel plates, applying oils and clearing the machine of impediments. He approached the machine as though it were a dangerous foe.

It took a while to realise he wasn't drunk at all. He seemed rough in speech. He was sober, but had a restless spirit and boundless imagination. Conversation with him was difficult. He was liable to misunderstand the simplest thing you said. His companion, Sancho, seemed the only person who could calm him down. We asked Sancho to get him to drop his machete. But Sancho too had diabolical notions about the printing machine. We had two mad people in that tight space.

There have been many accounts of what happened when Don Quixote stumbled into the first printing workshop he had ever encountered. Most of the accounts are lies. When an event passes into legend more people always claim they were there at the time. I was there when it happened. I was there.

'Let me see how it works!' Don Quixote commanded, waving the machete close to my chin.

He stood over the machine, his eyes flashing. I noticed his beard for the first time. It was long and white and pointed. His eyes had great vigour. His proximity made the space around him charged. What it was charged with I cannot say.

'What would you like to see?' I asked.

'Print something.'

'Anything?'

He gave me a sharp look.

'Yes.'

I continued printing what was on the blocks. I worked laboriously, sweating under the ferocity of his eyes. It was hard to work while he breathed down my neck. Eventually I pulled out some freshly printed pages.

'You have to wait for them to dry,' I said.

'I will wait.'

He still had the machete. His eyes made you think he was mad.

For him, waiting involved a special passion. I had never seen anyone wait with such intensity. It was as if by the force of his spirit he was regulating the motions of the moon or the subtle energies that flow through all things. When a person is touched by greatness might it not be because they are resonating with this subtle energy that runs through spider's webs and the intricate motion of the stars?

While he was waiting I noticed that he was concentrating on a shield of cobwebs in a high corner of the workshop. I was ashamed of the state of the place, and became defensive.

'We clean the place once every we–'

He cut through my explanation with the sword of his wit.

'If only,' he said, with a glint in his eyes, 'if only we knew the webs that connect us it would be easier to send a message to the highest authorities with a tug of thought than by protesting at their gates.'

He must have noticed the blankness of my look.

'I believe that the true warrior acts on the secret foundations of things, don't you?'

I gave him a look of incomprehension. The level at which he spoke was too elevated for me. Then I noticed something else about Don Quixote. He was a walking encyclopaedia of nonsense and wonders.

While waiting he began a dissertation on the analogies between the spider's web and people's inability to alter the world. He philosophised while we waited. I couldn't make out much of what he said. I heard fall from his lips words like Amadis of Gaul, Plato, the Knights of the Arduous Road. He mentioned the tragedies of Sophocles, the last ironic paragraph of *Things Fall Apart*, and a fragment of Okigbo which he quoted over and over again. Then he let fall a string of Luo proverbs, incanted a Swahili song, and strung out an Urhobo fable from which he drew threads of a luminous wisdom that held us spellbound.

When something extraordinary is happening in your life, time has a way of becoming an underwater phenomenon. It may be the distance of forty years, but there was a curious charm about those hours. It was a charm tinged with the old African magic that one rarely encounters. Sometimes one comes upon a seer emerging briefly from a long solitude in the forest. Don Quixote was like one of those seers. Like a story made real for a moment, he came into our lives, and then he was gone.

Afterwards all one heard of him were legends. He had waged battles with corrupt government officials, and embarked on campaigns in the forests of the North where Boko Haram terrorised the nation. It was even rumoured that he had been selected to join a resettlement programme on Mars. These are stories his madness generated. It is hard to say whether his deeds exceeded our imagination, or whether we are poor reporters of the marvellous.

Let it be said, while I have breath, that he made us more imaginative, just by being himself. I had never felt myself more locked in the box of my possibilities than in the presence of that man. He was a call to greatness. We failed to take up that challenge, cowards that most of us are. That failure is the lingering regret of my life. For a life passes, a life is lived. It is lived under fear and caution. One thinks of one's family. One thinks of one's self. But the life passes. And it is only the fires that your life lit in other people's souls that count. This I know now in the long, uneventful autumn of my life. There are some people one should never have met, because they introduce into your heart an eternal regret for the greater life you did not live.

The paper dried, and when I was satisfied Don Quixote would not have ink smudges on his face, I let him have what we had been printing. I did not know it would have the strange effect that it had.

He read the text very slowly. In all my life I have not met anyone who read more slowly. This puzzled me. It was because of reading too many books that he lost his mind. He couldn't have read so many books if he read so slowly.

'You are taking so much time,' I said to him.

The tension in the room changed. Sancho Panza, leaning his fat frame against the door, gasped. I did not understand the gasp and turned towards him. Then I felt the machete whizzing past my face, a cool breeze at the end of my nose. How calmly we regard extreme things after they have happened. I turned to Don Quixote. He had manipulated his face into a most peculiar shape.

'Do you think,' he said, 'that I read sixty-seven thousand three hundred and twenty-two books by taking instructions from you in how to read?'

The manner in which he spoke confused me. He made words sound more than they are. Other people say words and they mean less. He makes words feel like more. He makes your hairs stand on end when he speaks. I felt a furry growth at the side of my face when he addressed me. I stared at him, mesmerised.

'So you presume to tell Don Quixote how to read?'

My mouth was dry.

'Pull up your ears! Clear them of wax! Get rid of that dim expression! Stand up straight, young man, and listen!'

I drew breath. I felt faint. With a few syllables he could induce madness. His speech rocked the back of my skull. I don't know what came over me. One after the other, I pulled my ears. I tweaked them up straight like a rabbit's. All the while he stared at me with terrifying concentration. If he had gone on longer I might have gone up in flames. I made an effort to stand up straight, till my head grazed the ceiling of his contempt.

'What did I say?' he bellowed. 'Listen!'

I swallowed. It was a bruising adventure to be in his presence.

'In the course of a fifty-year reading career,' he said, directing at me an unblinking focus, 'I have experimented with three hundred and twenty-two modes of reading. I have read speedily like a bright young fool, crabbily like a teacher, querulously like a scholar, wistfully like a traveller, and punctiliously like a lawyer. I have read selectively like a politician, comparatively like a critic, contemptuously like a tyrant, glancingly like a journalist, competitively like an author, laboriously like an aristocrat. I have read critically like an archaeologist, microscopically like a scientist, reverentially like the blind, indirectly like a poet. Like a peasant I have read carefully, like a composer attentively, like a schoolboy hurriedly, like a shaman magically. I have read in every single possible way there is of reading. You can't read the number and variety of books I have read without a compendium of ways of reading.'

He stared at me and I felt he could see the inside of my head.

'I have read books backwards and inside out. I began reading Ovid in the middle and then to the end and then from the beginning. I once read every other sentence of a book I knew well and then went back and read the sentences I missed out. We are all children in the art of reading. We assume there is only one way to read a book. But a book read in a new way becomes a different book.'

I felt he was reading me as he spoke.

'And you have the nerve to tell me I am reading slowly. Part of the trouble with our world, my snooty young friend, is that the art of reading is almost dead. Reading is the secret of life. We read the world poorly, because we read poorly. Everything is reading. You are trying to read me now.'

His focus on me made me nearly jump out of my skin. I could not read him. I would not even dare to begin. He was like a Chinese character or a hieroglyph.

'Don't deny it. I can see your eyes wandering about my face as if it were an incomprehensible text.'

He paused.

'You are even trying to read this moment in time. But you read it dimly. The words are not clear on your pages of life. Youth clouds your seeing. Emotions pass in front of the text before you have grasped it. Can you read yourself in the chapter of time?'

He was staring at me again and all I had was muteness.

'You are a living paragraph of history. Around you are all the horrors of time and all the wonders of life, but all you see is an old man reading with all his soul. Do you know what I am reading?'

I shook my head, as if in a trance.

'I am reading a text by a Spaniard about my adventures in La Mancha.'

He guessed at the vacuity of my grasp.

'You have no idea what I am talking about, and you dare to criticise how I read?'

Another short laugh burst out of him.

'I don't read slowly. And I have long ago left reading fast to those who will continuously misunderstand everything around them. I read now the way the dead read. I read with the soles of my feet. I read with my beard. I read with the secret ventricles of my heart. I read with all my sufferings, joys, intuitions, all my love, all the beatings I have received, all the injustices I have endured. I read with all the magic that seeps through the cracks in the air. Do you, therefore, dare to judge the way I read?'

'I'm sorry, sa,' I murmured. 'I did not mean anything . . . '

'You would prefer me to gulp words down like a drunk guzzling palm wine in a bukka?'

'No, sa.'

'I suppose you think the faster you read, the more intelligent you are?'

'Not at all, sa.'

In truth though, this is what I believed.

'I suppose for you living fast is genius. I bet you fuck fast too. Fuck so fast that the poor woman has hardly had time to notice that you were in her.'

'Not at all, sa!'

'Not at all, what?'

'I don't know, sa. I am confused, sa.'

He conferred on me another long stare. I felt myself shrink to a tiny form, one inch from the floor. At the same time I felt magnified beyond the sky. He had that paradoxical effect. As he stared at me it seemed my life rushed before my eyes. I felt myself hurtling through time. I grew older, more arrogant, more successful. A chance event brought me down. Then the years of doubt followed. My waist thickened. I found a wife, became a father, and lost all my dreams. I worked hard, under the name of raising a family. And then I was an old man on a porch, wondering where all the magic and promise of life had gone. When only yesterday I was a young apprentice with all the world before me. Then Don Quixote comes to the printing workshop, and shakes my life with his mad Urhobo gaze.

'What you don't understand,' he said, relentlessly, 'is that nothing is done faster than when it is done well.'

For the first time, I noticed the unnatural silence in the workshop.

'You read for information, I read to extract the soul of the conception. Reading is like the mind of the gods, seeing beyond the page. Can you read an entire history from a single glance? Can you deduce a poet's health or the station of their time here on earth from a single line of poetry? You think reading is about reading fast. But reading is about understanding that which cannot be understood, which the words merely hint at.'

He would have gone on, in this fashion, had Sancho Panza not sneaked a look at the text that Don Quixote had in his hands.

'My dear Don,' said Sancho, 'but I see your name on the pages you are reading. How did that come to be?'

Don Quixote paused in a particularly brilliant crescendo of thought. Then he lashed Sancho with one of those gazes perfected in the creeks of Urhoboland.

'Did you not hear one word I've been saying to our young friend here about reading?'

'Don, the things you say are too intelligent for me. They go clean over my head. I watch them sailing past. I don't think it helpful to pay attention to what you say. But your name on these pages, what is it doing there?'

Don Quixote brought the machete, flat surface down, hard on the edge of the printing machine. Sparks shot out into our faces. Don Quixote was himself taken aback by the sparks. His eyes protruded. I could sense another long speech coming on. To distract him, I said:

'Aren't you going to continue with your reading?'

For a moment he seemed torn between a scientific and a literary choice. With a sigh, and pulling at his beard as if it helped him concentrate, he returned to the text. He read in silence like a man drowning. A wall-gecko ran halfway up the wall. The wall-gecko saw Don Quixote reading and was transfixed by the vision. I watched the wall-gecko watching Don Quixote. It must have been a historic sight.

Now, many years later, I see how much of a historic moment it was. It was a moment in which a golden line between the old and new time was crossed. Can someone reading constitute a significant moment in the cultural life of a whole people? Can something so intimate have historical repercussions? I do not want to make extravagant claims for such a subjective activity. But what if the understanding of one mind precipitates the understanding of the many? There is a moment in the life of a people when things are suddenly seen for what they are. It may be injustice, or it may be a great social evil. But what if such a seeing was achieved first by one and then by the rest of us? Maybe the great historical moments, the storming of barricades, the tearing down of palaces, are the outer form of an inner activity. Maybe a people see first and then the realm of deeds comes after.

But as Don Quixote read that text we could feel the air in the room change. His way of reading was like a prosecution of all our assumptions. It was like a thousand question marks scattered across our corruption-infested landscape. Even his face kept altering as he read. His beard was twisted into the enigmatic shapes of ancestral sculptures.

In the silence a thousand questions began to swim up to me. Maybe it was that long in-between time usually given up to chatter. Maybe it was the time used in covering up that which we do not want to see, but which stares at us like a corpse at the side of the street. Maybe it was that silence, so rare in our times, that allowed the questions to rise up to the holes in the roof, through which they escaped out into the nation.

Being an eminently practical man, according to his own curious logic, Don Quixote would disapprove of such fanciful notions. But something happened in that space, in that silence, as he sucked in the air with the concentration of his reading. It may have been the beginning of our reading the world that we saw all around us, the world that we suffered every day. It was that more than anything.

He infected us with a new way of reading. We began to read the cockroaches. We read the spider's webs. We read the raw roads and the corpses under the bushes. We read the cracks in our faces, through which despair seeped out. We read our extraordinary talent for evasion. We read our breathing and noticed what a pungent text the air made. When we began to read the shacks, the slums, and the palatial houses with armed guards and high electric fences, when we began to read those who grew fatter as we grew thinner, when we began to read the ambiguous text of our recent history, we saw that the world was not how we thought it was. Before we had seen the world as somehow inevitable. We had seen that it was the only way it could be. Now, with the new reading, we saw that the world was only one of a thousand ways it could be. But we had chosen this one, with its bad smells, its injustice.

All this happened in the space of a printed page. He read the page. Then took up another printed page. He read that. Then he looked up. His head aslant, he regarded us with puzzlement.

'What is it?' Sancho said, rushing forward. He sensed distress in the eyes of his beloved master and friend.

'What is it? What is it? Have you seen what I am reading?'

'No. What is it?'

I don't know how, but he had ink on his face. He looked both comical and ghoulish. He misunderstood our collective stares. He seemed to think that we knew what he had been reading, and that we had somehow colluded in it. His machete rose above his head, and we backed off into the shadows, and pressed ourselves into the walls. The shape of our backs ought to have dented the bricks.

'These are pages about our adventures,' he cried.

'What adventures?'

'All our adventures.'

'All?'

'All since we left Ughelli and roamed the world as far as La Mancha, fighting demons, defeating giants, rescuing women from abduction, tilting at oil rigs, battling corruption. It's all here!'

'But how can that be? No one else knows of those adventures except us. I haven't told anybody. Have you?'

'Don't be silly, Sancho.'

'But who is writing down those adventures? Is it someone we know?'

'Someone called Ben Okri. He claims to be writing the adventures from oral history.'

'Oral history?'

'Yes, oral history. Don't look so stupid, Sancho. It is word-of-mouth history.'

'You mean gossip?'

'Not just gossip.'

'You mean rumour?'

'No. Stories told by people.'

'Can you trust it?'

'Oral history can be more reliable than written history.'

'You don't really believe that, do you?'

'Why not?'

'People exaggerate. They tell tall tales. Sometimes they engage in propaganda.'

'I know. But oral history gives us the spirit, whereas written history gives us only the facts. The facts, by themselves, tell us very little.'

'So are we to believe this Ben Okri?'

'He also claims to be writing the adventures from manuscripts originally written by Cervantes, who wrote his from papers he discovered by Cide Hamete Benengeli, who got it from an Arabic manuscript.'

'It sounds very complicated.'

'It is not complicated at all. It's like Biblical genealogy.'

'What is genealogy? You are always using words bigger

than me and I am a big man. Can you not find a simpler word for a plain man like me?'

'And that is not all,' roared Don Quixote, ignoring Sancho's request.

'There's more?'

'Of course there is more. Why else would I be so upset?'

'You are always upset about something. Or you are always upsetting something.'

'Shut up, Sancho.'

Sancho offered the Don a glum look.

'This fellow has written adventures I haven't had yet.'

'You mean he has written your future?'

Don Quixote considered this. His face was almost meditative.

'He has written one future.'

'How many futures are there?'

'We have a wise saying in our village. A man's future changes when he changes how he lives.'

'Forgive me for being stupid, but is that not one of the futures too?'

'No!' bellowed Don Quixote. 'We believe that a person can confound their future. It was prophesied for me that I would die in my bed, and that I would renounce the life I have lived. But I will do no such thing.'

'How do you know?'

'They can write my future. But I am the only one who can write my present.'

'So you are going to become a writer now?'

'Of course not, Sancho. I have chosen to live. I have chosen the noble path of adventure, not the sedentary art of writing.'

'You had me worried for a minute.'

'When I say I will write my present I only mean that I will write it in how I live it. For many writing is what they do on a page. For a rare few, writing is what they do with life. Some write their texts on paper. I write my text on the living tissue of time. I write my legends on the living flesh of the present moment.'

'I prefer pounded yam and egusi soup, with goat meat.'

'Of course you do, Sancho.'

'Each to his own.'

'For me, however, all destiny is here. In this moment. This present moment is one the gods have no control over.'

'Why not?'

'Because they have yielded to us the marvels of consciousness.'

'I had never thought of that before.'

'Of course you hadn't, Sancho. Most people read books; I read life. Some people write stories; I live them.'

He looked around the workshop.

'Let's go,' he said abruptly. 'We have spent enough time in this house of embalmment.' He slid the machete into a rough sheath that he wore on his side.

Moved to a defence of my apprenticeship as a printer's assistant, I cried:

'Embalmment?'

'Yes, embalmment,' replied Don Quixote, calmly. 'What else are you doing here but burying living time in the tomb of print? What are you doing but fixing in the amber of print that which was fluid and multi-dimensional?'

Again I stared at him stupefied. My mind had a thousand objections, but my mouth was stuck. He continued evenly.

'This workshop is a graveyard of life. Life has a thousand colours, meanings, layers, aspects known and unknown. Print has only one face. That face, in a thousand years, is taken to be the only truth. This is a house of the falsifications of time. I will have nothing more to do with it.'

'But we leave a record,' I cried. 'This is history!'

'The father of lies!' returned Don Quixote with unnatural tranquillity.

The years pass and a great ambiguity falls over those words. The years pass and I become aware that we never really see what is there before us. It is as if the event veils its own truth.

It seems he could indeed read the future in a grain of text. The truth is that after he left that day we scoured all the printed matter we had in the shop. We found that nothing we had printed that day or any other day bore any resemblance to what he claimed he had read.

It began to dimly occur to us that maybe we did not know how to read the secret scripts of life concealed in the ordinary stuff we printed every day. It occurred to us that we did not know how to read at all. This was perhaps the greatest shock. Don Quixote had read our walls, the dust at our feet, and had discerned that which we would not notice in a hundred years. In that way he taught us that there is a secret reality before us all the time. This secret reality reveals all things.

There still remains some doubt as to whether his reading of this secret reality is a consequence of his madness, or whether our inability to read it is a consequence of our dimness. It may just be that we are blind to the prophecies written on the plain features of our times.

That day, after he returned the printed pages back to me, he cast one last look at the workshop. Did ever a glance reveal the poverty and richness of a place? For a moment, seeing it through his eyes, I wanted to tear down every brick from that squalid workshop. But then, seeing it through his eyes the next moment, I glimpsed an unsuspected magnificence. With his unique seeing he could transform a hovel into a castle.

After that ambiguous gaze, he turned to me. I expected from him a long speech, such as antique knights are

inclined to give. I braced myself for meandering locu-
tions. Instead he favoured me with a smile, in which was
mixed compassion and amusement. To this day I have
not been able to fathom the full meaning of that smile.
It bothers me often on the margins of sleep.

With a gesture to Sancho, he left the room. I should
write that line twice. No one has ever left a room the
way he did. He left it altered forever. He left the room,
but the room retained the stamp and magic and chaos
of his spirit. Afterwards when I went to the workshop a
little of Don Quixotism invaded my quiet life.

Why else do I write with elegiac cadences of a moment
that happened more than forty years ago? I too would
have liked to have set out on a steed and take on the
challenges of our times. Later we heard how he would
attack garage boys thinking they were stragglers from
Boko Haram, or would defend a prostitute in Ajegunle
thinking her a celebrated Yoruba princess, or how he
set upon a convoy of soldiers, accusing them of electoral
fraud. In the last instance he was beaten within a half-
inch of his life for his absurd bravery.

These actions have changed in the telling into deeds
of heroism that shame our famous activists. His deeds,
reimagined by our storytellers, made my days into something a little glorious. The years have been good to him.

When he died, in a hovel on the edge of the ghetto,
surrounded by his beloved books, he had only Sancho
with him, and a scheming niece. His last words were not

remembered. Sancho was too broken by grief to ever speak of them. But over the months word went round of his passing. All the market women he had irritated, all the politicians he had insulted, all the prostitutes he tried to reform, all the truck-pushers he had taunted, all the bus drivers who flinched when they saw him, all formed processions along his street and held long vigils outside his house.

I speak of these things with too much compression. They ought to be a thousand pages in the telling. But these are hurried and heated times. It is a wonder one can tell any story straight.

What happened with the rest of his life has been retold by many people. They are fleas on the back of a free-roaming bull. I only wanted to tell of one moment and its long aftermath. It is by the aftermaths that we must truly judge greatness.

He left the printing workshop that day and was struck by the muggy light of that Ajegunle sun. Outside stood the scrawniest donkey I had ever seen. It was flea-ridden and refractory. Don Quixote leapt on the donkey, and was immediately thrown. He picked himself up and dusted himself down. He turned to us and said:

'It seems Sidama does not want to be ridden today.'

He picked up the rope round the donkey's neck. That donkey was a rangy, stubborn thing. It looked as if it didn't think much of its master. Don Quixote kept coaxing it. He spoke to the brute as if it were an intelligent human being. A crowd had gathered to watch the strange sight of a man trying to reason with a donkey.

Then something unexpected happened. While Don Quixote was whispering into the donkey's twitching ear, Sancho gave the beast a short solid kick in the rump. After that the donkey became tame. Don Quixote looked at us as if to confirm the efficacy of his technique.

'All you have to do is reason with them,' he said.

He took up the halter, and rode towards the red cloud gathering in the north.

MIR ASLAM OF KOLACHI

Kamila Shamsie

In the city of Kolachi there lived the last of the Qissa-Khwans, or Storytellers. Once, the grandest boulevards of his nation were named for those of his vocation, but now only the peeling apartment block overlooking the sea, in which he had occupied the top-floor flat for decades, was known as Qissa-Khwani, though its official name as chosen by the building's owner was Paradise View. The surrounding buildings, also owned by the same man, had names such as Paradise Homes, Paradise Point and Paradise Point II, Paradise, and Paradise Itself, so, to avoid confusion, the locals assigned an unofficial name to each structure, of which Qissa-Khwani was the best known.

Mir Aslam, the last of the Qissa-Khwans, had been trained by his grandfather to recite the love stories which had kept his family in business for generations – stories of Laila Majnu, Sassi Punnu and Yousuf and Zuleikha – but as a young man caught up in a country's independence movement he had understood there were other kinds of stories people would pay to listen to – stories, first, of fighting the British, then of fighting the Indians, then of fighting military dictatorships, then of fighting other political parties. No government ever arrested him because each understood it would be easier and more fruitful to hire him to write his rhyming-couplet stories in their favour, which he would declaim to great effect at party conferences or during independence day celebrations. But since the boom in cable television at the start of the new millennium, the government's desire for rhyming couplets had fallen away – Mir Aslam was a man of the stage, not the screen – and as old age approached, the last of the Qissa-Khwans found himself in a state of professional crisis. It isn't that no one approached him anymore to commission stories, but that increasingly the world of public declamation was becoming a place for those who wanted tales of violent jihad.

Mir Aslam retreated into his books, refusing all commissions in which a drop of blood was spilled in the name of religion, and dreamt of a golden age of Islam in which scholars such as he (he had never been to university but was in possession of several honorary doctorates) earned their living through knowledge (as the world grew darker around him, Mir Aslam's learning grew in his own estimation – he even began to think those honorary doctorates in his possession had been conferred on him rather than bought in the Paper Bazaar). He dreamt, in short, of Qurtaba, in al-Andalus. There was no melancholy as beautiful as that brought on by those dreams of the capital of Muslim Spain, 'the ornament of the world', with its libraries, its translators, its book buyers who travelled the world in search of knowledge that could enrich that city in which 'books were more eagerly sought than gold or concubines'. At first, Mir Aslam dreamt that he was official storyteller to al-Hakam II, the most cultured of all the caliphs; when al-Hakam's eyes tired of reading but his thirst for stories remained unquenched he would call his Storyteller to his palace in Madinat al-Zahra, and Mir Aslam would be to him as Scheherazade to Sheharyar but without the fear of execution. The more he dreamt himself into the tenth century the more he yearned to set foot in what remained of Qurtaba – to taste the oranges, to sit on the walls of Madinat al-Zahra and see the world spread out beneath him, to walk barefoot beneath the arches of the Great Mosque and know that faith and art and a generosity of spirit could entwine so beautifully.

On the day the mosque he had attended as a child was bombed for being a home of worship to the wrong sect, he decided it was finally time for the pilgrimage to Qurtuba, and changing out of his ink-stained shalwar kameez into a suit and tie he set off for the travel agency next to the photocopier stall. One wall of the travel agency was covered in pictures of tall buildings hulking together, another had the holy Ka'aba surrounded by rings of humanity. Behind the desk a woman with talcum powder not fully blended into the wrinkles of her neck asked how she could help him. At first neither al-Andalus

37

nor Qurtaba made any sense to her. When he explained, she threw the word Schengen at him. Neither of them wanted to be inexplicable to the other so further efforts were made and finally he understood that he would need a visa to a place named Schengen – which was to Spain as al-Andalus was to Qurtuba – and in order to get the visa he must first buy a plane ticket and rent a hotel room, but there was every likelihood he would be refused the visa which meant he mustn't buy the cheap plane tickets which were non-refundable but the most expensive sort. As for hotel rooms, those could always be refunded but, the woman advised, leaning close enough that he could smell the talcum powder, that didn't mean he should rent a room at a very expensive hotel because that would make the visa officers suspicious.

When he asked if he had to pay her extra to issue a visa along with the ticket she sighed, looked at the nail polish bottle on her counter and then at him, as if deciding which was a better way to spend her afternoon, and then decisively dropped the nail polish bottle into a drawer. He would have to apply in person at a drop-off centre, she said, but she would help him with the application forms. But first he had to tell her which category of visa he needed. Tourist, Family, Medical Visit, Business, Conference, Diplomatic, Official, Airport Transit or Sailors' Transit. None of the above wasn't an option, and after listening to his reasons for the visit she suggested Tourist. Mir Aslam didn't like the sound of that;

it conjured up images of people who travelled in order to take pictures of themselves in places to which other people travelled in order to take pictures of themselves. He pointed to the wall with the photograph of the Ka'aba, and asked what visa was required for those who went on Haj. A pilgrimage visa. That was what he wanted for Qurtuba. She pulled up her neckline, pursed her lips. Pilgrimage is for the Holy Places, she said. Neither the government of Spain or Pakistan accepts your category. When she opened the desk drawer and removed the nail polish he understood he was dismissed. He was halfway down the street when he heard her voice, and returned to take the envelope full of paper that she handed to him.

Mir Aslam returned home, changed back into his indoor clothes, brewed an extra-strong cup of tea, and sat down at his desk which overlooked the dark-grey sand and dove-grey sea of Kolachi. First, the list of require-ments. A passport, valid for three months past his date of return from Spain. Mir Aslam had last required a passport nearly forty years earlier when he was flown out to London, UK, to perform at an exiled politician's birthday. A new passport would have to be acquired, but what was he to do about the next requirement, which was to also bring *all* previous passports, along with photocopies of all pages bearing visas and stamps? He consulted his English dictionary in case 'all' might mean 'the most recent' in some archaic version of English that was still spoken in Spain, but this seemed not to be the case. Not that it made a difference since he had neither his previous passport nor the ones before it, but what a strange requirement that 'all' was. It was the sort of thing that might deter many applicants, and perhaps someone should relay this to officials who made up rules without realising the consequences. Well, anyway, he would simply tell the officials about that period of his life in which he read a great deal about the Sufi ascetics and dispensed with anything that might seem excessive. He would offer to bring them to his house so they could see that aside from his books he owned almost nothing, and certainly didn't keep hold of old passports or any documentation related to travel. Perhaps they'd be too busy to visit, and he would arm himself against this eventuality by taking along pictures of the filing cabinets which had come with this apartment, and which he used to store tea and rice and lentils.

Next on the list was two recent passport-sized photographs – he patted his still-thick hair, and decided he would need a haircut first. The following requirement was 'accreditation of profession', defined as an 'introductory letter by the employer', which asked for such details as salary, period of work in the present organisation, or position or post in the organisation. Mir Aslam slumped in his chair, defeated. How far al-Andalus had fallen that it could not conceive of storytellers and poets and musicians, let alone pilgrims. Only tourists and the salaried could apply. Nowhere in the list of requirements did it say: tell us about your love for Spanish history, literature, dance, or those small green salted peppers he had once eaten at a Spanish restaurant on that visit to London, UK.

And what was this? They wanted his travel itinerary. Did Ibn Battuta have a travel itinerary when he visited Granada in 1350? No! He set off from Tangier intending to join the Moroccan army which was defending the Port of Gibraltar against the expected attack by Alfonso XI of Castile, but when he arrived he discovered the Black Death had killed Alfonso and so he turned his purposes from military to exploratory, wandering towards Málaga where orange trees grew in the courtyard of the mosque, and proceeding from there to Granada where the sultan's mother sent him a purse of gold coins in recognition of his status as a man of knowledge. Why shouldn't he, Mir Aslam, explain to the visa officials that he was a modern-day version of Ibn Battuta, whose travel itinerary would have read 'wherever my feet and the tides of history take me'? Yes, he would explain all this, and he would explain also that Ibn Battuta had no accreditation of profession beyond his own intellect and curiosity. And both these qualities Mir Aslam had, and would take along to the visa application centre.

The next day he returned to the travel agency. *She* was there again, her nails painted purple though yesterday's nail polish bottle had been a pleasing shade of pink, and seemed glad to see him. He had only intended to buy

41

the ticket and make the hotel reservations, which he'd failed to do the previous day when the matter of the visa came up, but she offered him a cup of tea and asked if he'd had any trouble with the application checklist, and he found himself talking to her about Ibn Battuta.

Was he a soldier, she asked, that he had set off to join the Moroccan army?

No, Mir Aslam explained. Ibn Battuta was everything that the moment demanded. He knew how to hold a sword, had used it in his travels, and when he heard the Moroccan army required reinforcements to hold Gibraltar against Alfonso he decided to join them.

And this Alfonso was Christian, she said? And Ibn Battuta was Muslim? So he was like those Muslims from Kolachi who went to fight with the Taliban when America attacked Afghanistan?

He most certainly was not! He was a Moroccan join-ing his nation's forces to repel invaders.

She shook her head at him. I wouldn't tell this story to the Spanish visa officials, she said. Can't you tell them you want to go to Spain to watch a bullfight? That will be much less suspicious than all this talk of jihadis who go where history takes them, and making a pilgrimage to the places where Muslims ruled over Spain. You think they want to be reminded of this?

It was a golden age of civilisation. Who wouldn't want to be reminded of that? And when they hear my story of it, they'll understand I value their country's history.

What story?

Mir Aslam stood up. The suit and tie felt wrong, but he would make do. He moved his chair to the centre of the room, and gestured for her to sit down in it, which she did when she saw he was adamant. Then he carefully cleared a space on her desk, and sat cross-legged on it, one hand raised in her direction in the formal storytelling pose. He had never done this in English before, but the Spanish visa official and he could exchange sympathetic comments about how they were both forced to communicate in English, that language of world domination, rather than in their more beautiful native tongues.

> Listen closely, sir, I am here to tell a tale
> Of Spain when it was a nation of Akbars, not Rafaels–

I don't think it's pronounced to rhyme with 'tale', she said. That tennis player, you know, with the muscles? His name is said in a way that rhymes with nothing.

In all his years as a Qissa-Khwan no one had ever interrupted to correct him. Interrupt to ask him to repeat a beautiful couplet, yes; interrupt with appreciative cries of *vah! vah!*, yes; interrupt to declare oneself an unworthy recipient of such poetry, yes. But interrupt to correct? Did she not see that in English he was like a sculptor of clay forced to work with cold, unyielding marble? Though he could not bend the material to his will, something of his deep knowledge of sculpture should still convey

43

itself beyond the superficial failures. Let her try to rhyme in English and see how far she would go! But he would not allow her taunts to shame him.

    Listen closely, sir–

How do you know it won't be a madam?

    Listen closely, please, I am here to tell a tale
    Of the golden age of Islam before it was derail

    Al-Andalus, Qurtaba, the wonder of Granada
    Let's not forget please Madinat al-Zahra

    Such libraries, such excellence,
        I must now shed some tears
    How further back we are now though
        forward in years

    Euclid, Homer, Aristotle
    Without the Moors would be forgotten

    What made it such a perfect mix,
    Islam and Spain? Was it the figs?

Figs? What do figs have to do with anything?
    In the Quran, Allah swears by the fig and the olive. Spain has both.

I think you're trying too hard to make this rhyme. Anyway, what is the point of all this? You think you can walk into a visa office and perform like this? First of all, you only go to deliver your documents to a courier company. They send them to the embassy. If the embassy wants to see you then you have to make an appointment with them, and there if you try to climb onto the official's desk they'll shoot you dead. But personally I think you'll be rejected straight away without an interview. Where is your letter from your employer?

Mir Aslam decided that a woman who could not appreciate the cleverness of an 'Aristotle / forgotten' almost-rhyme clearly lacked all understanding of the Qissa-Khwan's art and said could he please just buy his ticket. She asked for his passport, and he asked if his ID card would suffice.

I'm only doing this to win points for heaven, she said, and locked up the travel agency to accompany him to the passport office. In the back of the rickshaw they had to sit so close their sleeves touched, which made it too late to ask her name. She would have to be 'Madam' only.

Outside the passport office, men pressed forward towards the rickshaw in the way of those who could short-cut through long bureaucratic processes. At Madam's instructions, Mir Aslam handed one of them a certain amount of money and waited by the side of the road while Madam sat on a plastic chair beneath the shade of a tree. The man returned a short time later with a bank draft for an amount of money which was not too much less than the amount Mir Aslam had paid him – special discount, the man said, jerking his chin towards Madam.

Then he took Mir Aslam by the elbow and started to lead him towards the passport office. Mir Aslam looked back towards Madam, who was sipping a cup of tea. She raised a hand at him in a way that let him know she would be waiting. Inside the office there were many numbered counters. The man who had taken charge of Mir Aslam led him to the front of each line with a cry of My grandfather, he's unwell! which prompted everyone to move aside and let him through. At the first desk he handed in the bank draft, and received a slip of paper. At the next he handed in the slip of paper and received a plastic token; at the third, he had his picture taken (he had forgotten to have a haircut); at the fourth, they took his fingerprints and the plastic token. At the fifth they asked him for information that was already on his ID card and typed it into the computer. At the sixth they took his ID card and checked that what was written there matched what had been typed in by the person at the desk three feet away. At the seventh they printed everything out and a man handed him a pen, and said sign here, and here.

One signature was required at the bottom of the sheet, verifying all the information was correct. The other was required beneath a statement enclosed in a black box. Mir Aslam read the statement, in English and in Urdu. He looked up at Madam's man, who told him to sign and not worry about it. Mir Aslam read it again. It asked him to attest that people of a certain group were not Muslims, even though those people claimed they were.

What does this statement have to do with my right to travel? Mir Aslam asked. Madam's man told him not to speak so loudly. He guided Mir Aslam's pen hand towards the dotted line.

Mir Aslam stood up and walked out of the office. Madam stood up and came towards him.

Is it done? she said.

Do you have a passport? he asked.

Yes.

Can you explain to me, then. They said I should sign something on a form, something I don't understand.

Oh, she said. That. Yes. It isn't enough for the state to pass laws to say who is and who is not a Muslim; we must all agree with the state, and be complicit. Even when it's our own mother whose right to call herself a Muslim we are signing away.

Another man might have thought she was speaking in a general way, but he knew about voices, what they revealed and what they tried to hide – and he heard how the word 'mother' fractured as she spoke it.

Why must we agree? he said.

Otherwise no passport. Then we can never leave here, and never go to al-Andalus.

How can you go to al-Andalus if you kill the al-Andalus inside you to do it?

You didn't sign?

He shook his head, and she looked at him in a new way, a better way even than those audiences who shouted *vah! vah!* and begged him to repeat the best of his couplets.

Mir Aslam Khan, we live in a land without figs or olives. But at least we have men such as you.

She had checked to see his name in the second or two when his ID had been on her desk. He understood then why his grandfather, the wisest man he'd known, told him that no matter how the world might twist and turn there would always be an audience for the love stories of Laila Majnu and Sassi Punnu, and for men with more dreams than sense.

THE DOGS OF WAR

Juan Gabriel Vásquez
translated by Anne McLean

The same thing always happened: as the beginning of
the semester approached, and with it the class on *Julius
Caesar*, Osorio began to ask himself why he kept doing
what he did. This course he himself had invented was
just turning thirty-one; thirty-one identical years he'd
been shouting himself hoarse about Shakespeare to
law students, and he still hadn't managed to get them
to admire King Henry's Saint Crispin's Day speech, or
Iago's effective malevolence, or the fearful metaphors
with which Lady Macbeth attacks her husband's weak
points. At the beginning of 1984 – he remembered the
year very well; so many things had happened then –
Osorio had approached the dean of the university with
a proposal: a class that would teach future lawyers the
art of rhetoric using as a vehicle (that's what he'd said,
'vehicle') the great works of the Bard (that's what he'd
said, 'the Bard'). And here he was, thirty-one years later,
repeating the same course in the same order, letting a
scene from *Hamlet* lead to one from *The Tempest*, one of

Richard's speeches – he still found it moving to speak of graves, of worms and epitaphs – to those closing arguments of Portia's that every self-respecting lawyer should commit to memory. Today, walking south along Seventh Avenue, covering the twenty blocks between his empty house and the lecture theatre on foot, Osorio felt the uneasiness again, and said to himself that this would be the last time: next year there'd be no more talk of *Julius Caesar*.

Osorio had discovered that the students were less interested in Antony's rhetorical talent than in the story of the conspiracy and murder, and a few years earlier he'd decided that it was best to start with the sources. He devoted the whole first session to explaining how Shakespeare had practically copied Plutarch, and went through Julius Caesar's story as it appears in the *Parallel Lives*. The students then found out that the evening before his assassination, Caesar had been dining at the house of a friend, Marcus Lepidus, and at one point the guests had begun to discuss what the best way to die would be. Caesar was the first to answer: 'Unexpectedly.' They also found out that, according to Plutarch, Caesar had a bad night's sleep, not only because the bright moonlight shone into his bedroom, but also because Calpurnia was crying and moaning in her sleep, and at dawn confessed she'd been dreaming of him, of cradling his murdered body in her arms. Calpurnia asked Caesar to postpone his visit to the Senate, and he agreed; but someone asked him to think of what people would say if they knew that all-powerful Caesar postponed his commitments according to his wife's dreams. Caesar then allowed himself to be taken by the arm and led to the Senate; before entering, a Greek teacher called Artemidorus, who was familiar with some of the conspirators, tried to give him a warning note; but Caesar, swept along by the crowd, forgot the note or thought it unimportant. As he entered the Capitol, he recalled the prophecy – 'Beware the Ides of March' – and believed he had managed to evade it.

He took his usual place – beneath the statue of Pompey, the man who in life had been his fiercest enemy – and then the conspirators surrounded him. But Caesar suspected nothing: he thought they were approaching with petitions, as had so often happened before sessions began, and that's what they did at first, perhaps to conceal the threat. Then Metellus took hold of Caesar's toga and his insolent hands pulled the folds away from Caesar's neck, where a beating vein was bared. This was the sign. The conspirators advanced towards Caesar and unleashed the attack. Casca, whose sword fell on the back of the victim's neck, but without causing a serious wound, struck the first blow. 'O vile traitor, Casca, what doest thou?' said Caesar, and then all the conspirators drew their daggers and plunged them into the defenceless body. The last to do so was Brutus, leader of the plot, whose dagger penetrated so deeply into Caesar's groin that its blow alone could have caused his death.

Twenty-three stab wounds ended Caesar's life. Plutarch relates that the pedestal of Pompey's statue was running with blood; he also tells us that the rest of the senators fled in terror and that word of what had happened spread immediately, and the Romans shut their doors and windows and abandoned their shops. The conspirators also left, but they made a mistake: they left the body lying in the Capitol. The plan was to throw it in the Tiber, but in the clamour of the days that followed, levelled by fear, they never actually did. Antony, the friend who was most aggrieved by Caesar's death, had it carried through the Forum while he read Caesar's will, which left a generous amount of money to each Roman citizen, and the mutilated body, swollen and reeking, caused such an impression on the crowd that they surrounded it with tables and stools and burnt it right there. Then, taking firebrands, they went after the assassins with the intention of killing them and burning down their houses. They didn't find them, but something rotten was left in that flaming Rome, and the assassination of Caesar caused chaos and conflagrations and was the beginning of years of civil wars. And all this Shakespeare had stolen and put into verse, and for the last thirty-one years Osorio had raised his voice like a fist to say that those were the most beautiful, most precise and most eloquent words ever written about what happens in the world when a great man is murdered. But each year in that very same instant he realised his mind was playing that trick on him, that his memory (obstinate and wilful, always doing whatever it fancied) had begun to remember another great man who'd been assassinated.

The night of his death, Justice Minister Rodrigo Lara Bonilla was crossing the difficult city towards his residence in the north end, a brick house in a neighbourhood with a pastoral name: 'Recreo de los Frailes', or 'Friars' Playground'. He was sitting in the back seat of his white Mercedes-Benz, behind the driver, with some documents in his hands; at his side, accompanying him like silent passengers, were two books – *Life Sentence*, one was called, and the other, with a black cover, *Dictionary of the History of Colombia* – although Lara wasn't thinking about the books or the papers, but about what was happening to his family. Ever since the first threats, his wife had begun to run their lives the way people do when they are in danger. Their children had instructions not to answer the telephone, and if they did, not to say anything when asked if their father would be home soon or how many people he'd left with. Sometimes, when Lara answered, he heard a recording of a phone conversation he'd just had; other times, a voice gave him the exact address of his children's school and reminded him what they'd been wearing on the previous Sunday. Lara told them they were no longer allowed to go to the park. He had to live with the uncomfortable feeling of depriving his children of a normal existence, and that made him delight in the rare normality of the occasional moment. That's what he wanted to do when he got home: find a bit of lost normality or at least pretend not to know, as everyone knew, that right then in some part of Colombia a plan was being concocted to murder him.

That very morning a trusted colonel had told him: Pablo Escobar's men were going to kill him during his next trip to Pereira. The intelligence was correct, but what no one knew was that Escobar himself had initiated the rumours of the attack, and his objective was precisely to get the minister to stay in Bogotá. For months, Escobar's men in Bogotá had been following Lara relentlessly: they knew what time he left his house in the morning and what time he left the office in the evening, they knew his preferred route (the highway and 127th Street), and they also knew that two jeeps, each with four well-armed bodyguards, accompanied him, as well as another bodyguard in the front passenger seat of his car, on the driver's right-hand side. It wasn't an easy hit, but Escobar's subordinates had recruited new people, given them bullet-proof vests and weapons and two trucks to get around in, and found them a safe place to hide in Bogotá. This time they weren't going to fail.

The idea of assassinating Lara had been brewing for a long time, but not as long as the profound hatred

Escobar had for the minister. It had all begun years before, when Lara expelled him from his political movement in spite of the fact that Escobar, a man of a mysterious fortune, was constructing an entire neighbourhood to provide housing for 400 poor families, had installed sewer systems in godforsaken shanty towns, and had even attended Felipe González's inauguration in Madrid, invited by a Spanish business associate. For Escobar, the expulsion was an intolerable humiliation on the part of those scornful elites of Bogotá, those oligarchs in their suits and ties who'd managed the country's destiny since the dawn of time. Lara was also denouncing in the Colombian Congress the infiltration of drug lords' money into football, where teams served to launder the traffickers' dollars, and into politics, where congress-men were bought, laws and decrees designed and entire campaigns financed right under judges' noses. Lara uncovered the operation of that machinery of horror and gave the whole debate a resonant nickname: *hot money*. 'I know what to expect for denouncing gangsters, but that doesn't intimidate me,' he told journalists one day. 'If I have to pay for it with my life, so be it.' And then he went after Escobar.

He denounced him as a criminal who dressed in sheep's clothing to run for Congress. He accused him of starting a paramilitary movement called Death to Kidnappers. He calculated his fortune at five billion dollars and asked if it were possible, as Escobar claimed, that his money came from hard work and the luck of having won the lottery several times. Escobar then held his own press conference and, without looking at the camera, read a piece of paper demanding the minister present evidence of his accusations within twenty-four hours or he'd be sued for slander, and Lara not only repeated those accusations in Congress, but did so giving unknown details about the drug world, bringing reams of paper and wooden pointers into the oval chamber to explain, in his professorial voice while his indignant unruly hair fell over his forehead, the existence of drug laboratories the size of villages and flotillas of small planes exporting cocaine from the commercial runways of El Dorado Airport. Escobar was expelled from Congress; the United States government revoked his visa; in the Yarí River basin, the police raided labs and captured supplies, helicopters and 13.8 tons of high-grade cocaine. A few days later, Escobar called an urgent meeting at the Hacienda Nápoles. The heads of the cartels arrived at his house – passing by the hippopotami and patches of pink flamingos and the iron dinosaurs and the bullring – and they all ate well and drank aguardiente and put their agreed shares into a kitty of millions whose only objective was to organise, before this problem got out of hand, the assassination of Rodrigo Lara Bonilla.

*

No, it wasn't strange that Osorio should think of Lara
Bonilla now, walking across Parque Santander and passing Café Pasaje. Lara had been dead as many years as
he had been teaching his Shakespeare course: that July
day in 1984, as Colombia wept and wondered when it
had become possible for a gangster who fancied himself
a politician to murder a government minister, he was
preparing his lecture on *Julius Caesar* and the structure of
the rest of the course. (Should he include *Titus Andronicus*?
Should he put *Macbeth* before *As You Like It*? How much
work it had been.) Today the students were waiting for
him under the neon lights in the same methodical disar-
ray as ever, hectic teenage activities in the corners, the
sound of pages being readied for pens, but a solid silence
filled the room as soon as Osorio stepped onto the wooden
stage. He spoke, as he did every year, of three passages
from the work: first, Mark Antony's monologue in front
of Caesar's recently assassinated corpse; second, Brutus's
clumsy and prosaic speech, only saved from oblivion by
a nice antithesis ('not that I loved Caesar less, but that I
loved Rome more'); and third, Antony's brilliant reply:
those marvellous metonyms, those cutting epistrophes,
that lethal irony. But today there was a curious interest, a rare spectacle of attentive eyes and raised hands.
What was going on? It didn't surprise him that Señorita
Gómez, the best student he'd had in a long time, raised
her long tanned arm and asked if they could go back for
a moment to Antony's prophecies before Caesar's corpse.

57

No, said Señorita Gómez, it wasn't a simple prophecy, but a fully-fledged curse. And she read in Spanish with good diction and an attractive voice:

> Domestic fury and fierce civil strife
> Shall cumber all the parts of Italy:
> Blood and destruction shall be so in use,
> And dreadful objects so familiar,
> That mothers shall but smile when they behold
> Their infants quartered with the hands of war . . .

Listening to his words in his student's voice, Osorio felt secretly proud of the translation. He'd been improving it over the years, and now it seemed like a lifetime ago when he began with borrowed translations: that of Astrana Marín, for example, although later he preferred García Calvo's *Macbeth* and Tomás Segovia's *Hamlet*. At the turn of the century, when a number of years had passed since the car bomb at the Centro 93 shopping mall (and he'd gradually grown used to solitude and better knew how to contend with sadness), Osorio began to fill his time with his own efforts. He discovered that in this hard-fought grappling with the Bard's stubborn words hours would fly by unnoticed, and in those years that was exactly what he needed: for time to slip away and to forget about life. But he couldn't talk about any of this with his students, of course, and he wasn't even sure that these students would remember Centro 93, or any of the other bombs of that year either. So he rushed on with the class, and they spent quite a while talking about those lines and also, inevitably, the following ones:

> And Caesar's spirit, ranging for revenge,
> With Ate by his side come hot from hell,
> Shall in these confines, with a monarch's voice,
> Cry havoc and let slip the dogs of war . . .

Of course it was a threat, Osorio said to Señorita Gómez, but was that not, Señorita, what tragedy had done since the beginning of time? All tragedy, Señorita, is built upon these foundations: that the death of a great man can drag everyone else over the precipice. The first to put it into words was Chaucer, said Osorio: tragedy is the story of a man fallen out of high degree. First he needs to arrive at the heights, by birth or virtue, that is, he needs to be a person whose fate matters to the people. That's why, Señorita, men go to war to protect King Duncan, that's why they risk their lives to protect Hamlet, and that's why the results of Caesar's assassination are what they are: the death of a great man has consequences, Señorita, it produces domestic fury and fierce civil strife, produces blood and destruction and havoc, and drags defenceless citizens along with it. And there's nothing we can do to avoid it.

*

Escobar gave the job to two hitmen who had his utmost confidence, in spite of their youth and inexperience: Guizado and Velásquez. They were members of a gang known as Los Quesitos, and they'd learned to kill in the Sabaneta school, south of Medellín, where an Israeli mercenary taught teenagers with no future how to control a motorbike and how to shoot at moving targets from the awkward position on the rear rack. Fire in the shape of a cross, he advised his apprentices. You won't miss if you fire in a cross. These instructions were in Guizado's mind as he sat on the back of the red Yamaha, weaving in and out of the Bogotá traffic, holding onto Velásquez's jacket with one hand and constantly watching, over his shoulder, the position of the jeeps escorting the Mercedes-Benz; the only white Mercedes-Benz in the tunnel at that moment, the white Mercedes-Benz with the licence plates FD5883, memorised by both Velásquez and Guizado, the white Mercedes-Benz with the justice minister in its back seat.

From the motorbike, Guizado or maybe Velásquez saw it make a sudden manoeuvre to get ahead of the heavy traffic. It was an unexpected movement that one of the escorting jeeps, the white Toyota, didn't manage to follow; it was left behind, trapped in the traffic, while the minister's Mercedes advanced west, followed only by the grey jeep. The hitmen saw their opportunity: Velásquez gave chase to the Mercedes and Guizado raised the Ingram submachine gun and the windows of the

Mercedes shattered under the bullets, the side ones as well as the back. The bodyguards in the grey Toyota opened fire while Domingo, the minister's driver, accelerated without turning around, ducking his head between his shoulders and looking out through the steering wheel, maybe thinking he'd managed to get away. He didn't know that the murderers' motorbike, chased by the bodyguards and harassed by gunfire, had skidded on a difficult curve: Lara's murderer had turned suddenly to throw a grenade at the grey jeep and lost his balance; the wheels spun on the wet asphalt (it had been drizzling) and the bike took a violent tumble. Guizado died with his head smashed open on the road. Velásquez turned out to be an adolescent, almost a child; he was captured, handcuffed, and thrown into the back of a jeep, one of the bodyguards' or maybe a police van, the way you'd throw a bag of manure, and there he stayed, curled up in the foetal position, tied hand and foot, crying cowardly tears and begging them please not to kill him.

Meanwhile, Domingo arrived at Lara's house. The minister was unconscious in the back seat, and the bloodstain on the blue upholstery was dark in the night. The bodyguards had caught up by now and ascertained the gravity of the injuries. In the following days, the newspaper *El Tiempo* would publish a diagram to explain them, just a sketch with eyes and lines leading out to informative captions: 'In this spot one bullet was found,' you could read above an arrow pointing at part of the skull, just above the left eyebrow; other captions provided an inventory of the rest of the wounds: '1 bullet hole in the right arm, 1 bullet in the lung, 3 bullet holes in the cranium.' Those wounds were already fatal, but his bodyguards didn't know any of that yet when they pulled him out of the Mercedes and put him in the back of a van, nor could Lara's wife and eldest son, who, alerted by the shouts and sounds of engines and car doors, had come out into the front garden. They wanted to accompany him. They climbed into the van and were driven to the Shaio clinic, thirty blocks away. Dr Augusto Galán, who was on duty, saw Rodrigo first, the minister's eldest son, who arrived with his hair wet and his hands red with blood and a first aid kit clutched against his chest. The doctor's brother, Luis Carlos Galán, was a friend and co-founder of the New Liberalism movement, and nobody had to tell him what had just happened, because he'd feared it for a long time.

That evening, after class, Osorio arrived home worn out, with a dull ache in his shoulders, and couldn't resist pouring a dash of cognac into his coffee, as he used to do in the old days. He looked for the Arden edition on his desk, the one he'd been using lately, but soon set it aside, and took another three steps to find the sonnets. The well-worn little book opened at the usual place without Osorio having to run his fingers blindly over the edges of the pages. The day of his wedding, while the rest of the world flew about getting everything ready, Osorio had sat down in front of a dictionary and quickly translated those lines, and that improvised piece of poetry was his first gift to Antonia. Pablo Escobar had just put a bomb on an Avianca plane, killing more than a hundred people in an attempt to kill one politician, but the city had not yet accepted that years earlier, with the assassination of Lara, an all-out war between the cartels and the government had begun, and the city was its theatre. Even though bombs exploded everywhere, people carried on living. They carried on getting married, for example, as Osorio got married even though the DAS building, the police intelligence headquarters, was bombed, and carried on going out to parties and shopping and teaching classes about dead Englishmen even though other bombs exploded: the one at the Bulevar Niza shopping centre and the one at the Chamber of Commerce and especially the one at the Centro 93 mall, with its windows shattering into thousands of murderous splinters. 'Let me not to the marriage of true minds,' Osorio translated, 'admit impediments', and presented his Spanish version of the sonnet to Antonia that evening on their wedding night. She smiled as no one had ever smiled, and in the three years they were together – three years, one month and seventeen days, to be precise – learned it by heart, though she knew no other line by the Bard nor had any interest in knowing any. She didn't know, for example, a single line from *Julius Caesar*, not the one about the civil strife that is unleashed when a great man is assassinated, nor the one about Caesar's spirit crying 'havoc' like Pablo Escobar in that recording that would later come to light, that police recording of one of his telephone calls, the words of which Osorio knew by heart. 'We have to create real havoc,' says Escobar, and also orders his hitmen to sow 'civil strife', and to Osorio it had always seemed a curious coincidence, that Escobar should say 'havoc' just like Caesar's spirit, that Escobar should say 'civil strife' just like Mark Antony. On these coincidences or on his contemplation of them he has spent his time, and the truth is they've helped him not suffer so grievously for the woman who is no longer there, for the woman who will never come home, for the woman who went shopping at Centro 93 and found that someone had let slip the dogs of war.

CORIOLANUS

Yuri Herrera
translated by Lisa Dillman

Everyone in the room had committed atrocities, though
only Marcius acknowledged it out loud. 'I assume full
responsibility for what happened,' he'd said after his
boys cracked down on those who were now, once again,
rebelling in Corioli.

'No one's denying their right to pitch a fit,' he'd
added in private. 'That's what we're here for. But if
we didn't enforce order in the end they'd feed on one
another.'

First he'd sent a commission to tell the rebels to
accept what the government was offering: with that
compensation, each of them could open a corner store,
or squander the money and then still live well – the golf
course would provide jobs for everybody. And when
they raised their fists dramatically, Menenius, the head
of the commission, smiled with the wisdom of a man
who's beheld many a tantrum, and shared with them a
truth as clear as cash: 'Your knees, to them, will help,
not arms.' If they listened to him they might even get

a little lagniappe, a bit of land someplace where there was nothing to fight over, say. They hadn't listened.

Next Marcius had sent some lawyers to make them see that it had all been done in accordance with the law, that the only rights being infringed were those of the new owners whose land they were occupying, the papers were right there, couldn't they see? They hadn't listened to them, either.

Then he sent in the riot police under the instruction to show them what the State was made of if they so much as threw a stone. To his surprise, those ill-paid and worse-trained men had carried out their charge with inconceivable rage, as though their place in heaven were riding on it. Where others would have balked, they broke seventy-eight bones, killed four men and retook the land.

That was when Caius Marcius, government secretary, had said, with premeditated urgency, that he assumed full responsibility for what had happened, leaving the governor there like an adornment, or worse, a coward. The governor's abdication scarcely gave Marcius the time to make new calculations, but he didn't need time, what he needed was his hands untied and some-one to pass the wallet. Using the former he'd opened the latter.

That was why Menenius had come – walking in on the meeting between Marcius and Cominius – to tell him how the rebel negotiations had gone. He managed to overhear Cominius say, 'Problem with these deadbeats is they think they can piss in places their dicks don't reach.'

Marcius didn't bat an eye at the interruption, for Menenius had no need to knock, but Cominius cocked his brow a few millimetres.

'Menenius, sir. Long time,' he said.

Menenius bowed his head respectfully and glanced at Marcius.

'I'll come back.'

'Good, we're almost done here, Menenius.'

And he walked out of the office.

He didn't mind waiting. In his mind he ran through the speech Marcius would read before the rebels to seal the pact. And after that the governorship would be his, who would challenge him? It was a great day for Menenius too. He'd trained Marcius. Taught him to say one thing while thinking another. Shown him the doors and finally they'd got them open. There would be a great celebration that night, but he wouldn't go. He preferred to stay home, listen to some music, drink port.

He heard the men rise from their seats.

'That's that,' Menenius assumed. The new deal would be better for all: different land for the old owners, more land for the new owners. But they had to wait for things to calm down. That was why they'd sent the riot police to the station and Menenius to talk to the rebels. At least that's how they'd played it to Cominius.

(Cominius, too, had committed at least one atrocity, but he thought no one knew. Menenius never got his hands dirty, but every day he strangled the same subject over and over, every day, in his head.)

He remembered he had a dentist appointment.

They looked exhausted but not defeated. The difference between the two rebel representatives was that while one seemed anxious to find out what else they could get, the other looked like she was spoiling for a fight. Menenius was acquainted with both types: Aufidius was one of those who liked to proceed bit by tiny bit – a bit for his own pocket and a tiny bit to divvy up among the rest. Cunning man, but sensible: he believed in no one and nothing but the eloquence of the greased palm. Baranda, on the other hand, was so pure she was dangerous. People like her thought the only way to sow the fields anew was by burning the soil.

'If this land is really as good as you say,' Aufidius said, 'give us some guarantees; that's all we need.'

'It is,' said Menenius, 'and we will.'

'And compensation stays the same.'

'Not a peso less.'

He was looking at Aufidius but could feel Baranda's eyes boring through his skull.

'And you really think it's going to be that easy,' she said.

Aufidius looked at her in exasperation.

'We already voted on this in assembly.'

Baranda didn't even turn, just kept staring at Menenius.

'Tell Marcius to come sign.'

'If you go to the secretary's office, he'll be more than happy to commit in writing,' Menenius replied.

'Here, before us all.' Baranda pointed to the plaza.

Aufidius wavered for a moment, during which he seemed to be awaiting his instincts, and then said, 'Yes, tell him to come.'

Menenius nodded slowly.

'I'm sure the secretary will be very pleased to have you receive him.'

The moment he saw her walk in he knew Cominius had done something to her, but he still asked:

'How'd it go?'

'Fine.'

'When do you begin?'

His daughter shrugged her shoulders. Her hands trembled slightly.

'I don't know.'

Menenius approached and clasped her elbows.

'What happened?'

She was looking down.

'Like you said. I went to see if he'd give me a job and he said yes.'

'And?'

'That's it.'

'What do you mean that's it?'

'He gave me the job. But I'm not going to take it.'

'Why not?'

'Because. I don't want to.'

She jerked her arms to shake Menenius off and turned without looking at him. She wouldn't look at him again, because she knew he knew but chose to pretend he didn't.

'What happened?'

'Doesn't matter.'

The office door opened and the two men strode out. They clapped one another's backs noisily.

'Cominius, a pleasure as always.'

'Mr Governor, pleasure's all mine.'

'Easy, tiger; wait for the toast.'

And they both laughed. Cominius repeated, 'Mene-nius, sir,' as he passed Menenius, who in turn repeated his head-bowing. He waited for Cominius to disappear into the elevator before turning to Marcius.

'He took that pretty well.'

'Yes.'

Marcius was still staring at the elevator. He'd said yes but was thinking about something else.

'He took that pretty well,' Menenius repeated.

Marcius had said: 'This ass'll be our bargaining chip. We deliver his head to those roughnecks, and the second they're pacified we get other investors in. Faced with a done deal he won't be able to say squat. He's fucked. Didn't I promise you, Menenius? It was just a question of patience.' That was what he'd said.

'Turned out to be a crafty little bastard,' Marcius said. 'He smelled a rat and came with a counter-offer. Outbid the other investors, and we keep the difference.'

He turned to Menenius and put a hand on his shoulder.

'We need to get this through any way we can, and the second things settle down we hit him with all we got. Priorities, Menenius. You better than anyone know about those.'

Menenius didn't respond. He was trying to work out what was actually going on behind Marcius' pupils and hoping there was something true, despite experience telling him this was one of those promises he handed out like small change. And then:

'Of course. Priorities.'

Marcius turned to walk into his office and – without even looking back – asked, to confirm what he assumed:

'All taken care of with that lot?'

'Done and dusted,' replied Menenius.

Menenius had a near-pathological knack for remembering faces. He only had to see them once to file them away in his head, together with their names and the exact places he'd seen them. What he lacked, however, was Marcius' talent for convincing anyone that, in effect, he really did remember them. Marcius made whoever stood before him feel as if he'd been waiting for them all his life, he not only shook hands but strode toward whoever was holding theirs out with the determination of a man heading to a podium. He was so overconfident it was as if he were being adored by the masses at every moment, even those when no one was adoring him.

Menenius called his secretary on the private line.

'Alma, have they called off the riot police guarding the Palace?'

'Yes, sir, they're gone. Would you like me to put you through to the captain to have them called back?'

'No need, Alma dear, we don't need them. But do contact the Coriolans' little leaders. Tell them I'm on my way.'

'Right away, sir.'

'Oh, and Alma' – Menenius paused – 'happy birthday. Just make that one call and then take the day off.'

The rebels were in permanent assembly, Aufidius attempting to defuse the remaining objections and Baranda making it hard for him. They received him at the back of the auditorium.

'What time's he coming? The people are getting restless,' Aufidius said.

'Soon, very soon, we just need to fine-tune a few details,' Menenius said.

Both leaders opened their eyes wide. Aufidius in shock, Baranda almost jubilant. Menenius pulled from his briefcase a map he'd taken at random from his office and unfolded it before them.

'One small change. Rather than that land it's going to be this land. Tiny bit further but just as good.'

'This is unacceptable,' Aufidius said.

One of his men came to ask what was the matter, if they had a time yet, there had to be something he could give the people.

'I'll go tell them we're just working that out now,' Aufidius said. He turned to Menenius and gestured scornfully toward the map. 'We had a deal.'

Baranda and Menenius were left alone. She observed him with a twisted smile.

'So was Marcius the one who made this decision?' she inquired.

'What do you think?'

Baranda smiled openly.

'No turning back now . . . '

'Look, Baranda, Marcius, when he wants to be, is a tiger-footed fury; what matters is which side he's placed his fury on, yours or the other. But he knows how to listen.'

Baranda narrowed her eyes and tamped down her smile on hearing the final comment.

Aufidius returned, agitated.

'They're going to wait, but not for long. And they're not going to accept the changes.'

'Menenius here thinks if we go talk to Marcius we can persuade him,' Baranda said.

'Really?' Aufidius leaned anxiously toward Menenius.

'As I already told you, the secretary will be happy to receive you.'

'We agreed he was going to come here.'

'Marcius loves and respects you both, you know that, but don't force him to get into bed with you out in the open, in front of everyone. You've got to give a little.'

'They don't want us at the Palace. You're sending us to get the bum's rush.'

'The riot police are gone. Send a commission.'

All three remained silent.

Then Baranda said, 'The time for commissions has passed.'

She took a few steps toward the stage and announced to the assembly: 'To the Palace!'

Menenius peeked out from behind the curtains and pointed to a group heading for the exit, machetes in hand.

'I don't think that's necessary.'

'Of course not, Menenius,' said Baranda. 'But as you and your pretty words know so well, one never abandons one's tools.'

'Open your mouth wide, wider, wider,' said the dentist.

Now he'd start making small talk, like always, even though Menenius could only make throaty sounds in response.

'I'm going to give you a little anaesthetic,' he continued, 'just in case. All you'll feel is a tiny prick.'

Menenius had already begun to disengage, as he did every time the dentist made him mute. He was thinking about priorities, about loyalty, about acts of vengeance. He was thinking he couldn't judge Marcius for knowing what came first; nor did he believe himself reprehensible for having seen, suddenly, the sense of his own words. It was not, as he'd thought, the time to celebrate, but to see whom one's knees best served at the moment. Right now there was only one act of vengeance he could take.

He heard sounds out on the street. Shouting, machetes scraping against the ground.

'Feel anything?' asked the dentist. 'No, right? OK, now we can stick the knife in with confidence and you won't even wince. Ha! No, of course not. Just a drop of blood, at most.'

Menenius was trying to discern what was going on outside. He focused intensely, managed to put it into words and then throated them out, though only because he was sure the man with the knife in his mouth wouldn't understand:

'Hear that? Sounds like the waving of arms.'

GLASS

Nell Leyshon

The day I was born it was hot and airless. It felt as though the sky had been lowered and there was a new glass roof above the world, trapping in the heat.

My mother and father were working in the field when the pains began. They couldn't go back to the house because it was a thirty-minute walk away. And the house was another thirty-minute walk away from the village.

And so they went into the byre where the walls were three-feet thick and it was cool. My father broke open a clean bale of straw; my mother lay down and he knelt by her side. He had seen this unfold many times before, had urged many young out from the black and white flanks of his cows.

When I slipped out onto the straw, he wiped off the vernix, noticed the gash between my legs, handed me to my mother.

She named me Eve.

*

People make such a fuss about babies. They coddle them. Swaddle them. They hold them with great care, as though their bones are made of eggshell.

Mine are not.

When I was born my skull, like all our skulls, was pliable; it was made up of plates of bone connected by membranes. As I edged out through the birth canal, the plates shifted closer together to allow my passage. Then as I emerged into the air, they spread apart like the continents on the globe, settling into place.

On the front of my head the soft gap between the bones, the fontanelle, pulsated. The rhythm echoed my heartbeat.

It took eighteen months for the fontanelle to close, and for the skull to fuse.

I was a quiet child.

My mother later told me she never heard me cry. Not a peep.

I was an obedient child.

My mother sent me to school and as I walked through the door I didn't look back.

I was a curious child.

Curious: odd, a one-off, a quirk.

Curious: I needed to know everything.

My brain never stopped working. Thrum thrum. It worked so hard from morning till night that it felt hot within my skull. Only at night did it cool off.

*

Childhood is a curious place for a curious child. I was always an odd fit. Too small, too freckled, too pale and too clever. No one likes a clever person. No one likes a clever girl.

At first my father and mother tried to get me to work in the same field where I was born, but I was small and I was never strong. A farmer, my father liked to say, needs to be strong in the arm, thick in the head. I was the inverse: weak arms, strong mind.

I spent most days reading.

Until the age of eleven my world was unpredictable. The stairs led to other planets where I walked upon the sky, and the earth with her blue seas and green continents curved above me; under the table lived giant cats who curled into balls I could rest my head upon; my bed sailed oceans.

I thought this was how my world would always be, but no. In September, after a long summer, I was told it was time for the big school.

The freedom of the field was over and I was about to be channelled into the cattle crusher, the trap where I would be dehorned, deloused, branded.

I was about to find out that at a certain age if you still claim you can see fairies at the end of the vegetable patch, or that you can hear creatures howling and eating their young in the night, you are threatened with the head doctor who gives you medicine and wraps you in very tight bandages so your arms can't move.

The first day of school I walk into the village and catch the school bus. I climb up the three metal steps and sit on one of the seats at the front.

My feet don't touch the floor. My legs stick out.

I look like a doll. Freckled face, too-big clothes. Ankle socks with a lace ruff.

The other girls sit in pairs. They chatter like painted birds.

– Oh you look so lovely in that.

– I love that blue.

– Your hair. Look at your hair.

In the school I am told to sit and look towards the front of the class where various adults talk at me. I am supposed to listen, regurgitate, listen, regurgitate.

It isn't long before I realise that they don't know any more than me.

I let them know what I think.

I am not a popular student.

Days and months pass and one morning I climb onto the bus, book in hand, and take my normal seat. But my legs, instead of sticking out stiffly, touch the floor.

The week after that when I walk into the kitchen

my mother looks at me as though she has never seen me before.

People start to remark upon the state of my body:

– What have you been eating?

– Have you been sleeping in the greenhouse?

My legs start to hurt. The bones inside ache. Growing pains, the nurse says.

And then one morning I take off my night clothes to put on my day clothes. And I see more changes.

Where there was once arid land there is growth.

I grow a copse under each arm. A copse between the legs.

Deposits of fat begin to appear. I soften. I grow two small hills on my chest.

I am becoming a landscape.

The river water is blood.

I don't understand why they called me Eve. She was the first woman and had not come from another woman. She came from a rib.

I have pointed out the various inconsistencies in the story. I have asked why the first Eve is always portrayed as having a belly button. Where was the umbilical cord attached?

One day at school I am sitting on a wooden chair in the corner of an empty room. Chalk dust covers the floor.

I have a book in my hand and I am devouring it, page by page.

The door opens but I don't look up.

Footsteps come towards me but I don't look up.

A voice speaks:

– What are you reading?

My eyes never leave the lines, never look up.

– I said, what are you reading?

It is only then I realise I am being addressed. It is an odd feeling: someone has asked a question that expects an answer. It is not a taunt.

I look up.

His hair is the dark of a night after a waned moon. It falls over his face, allows him not to look another in the eye. He is from the farm in the valley and looks as though he has never seen the light. His skin is as pale as mine. He smells of cow dung, not unpleasant. It reminds me of home.

– The book, he says. – What is it?

I am obedient and turn the book over so he can see the spine. He reads the words.

– It's good, he says.

I feel a jolt through me. It is as though the words bear a current, an ability to stir me out of a deep sleep. There is only one way he would know if it was good or bad. He reads, too.

I look at him.

– I want to say something to you, he says.

I wait.

He takes a deep breath. His voice trembles. – I think you are pretty.

It is another jolt.

Pretty. Pretty. Me? White skin (so pale it's almost translucent), covered in specks of brown, like mud flicked up after a plough.

I stand up.

He asks me where I'm going.

I don't answer.

I need to go home. Now.

I slam the book shut and the chalk dust in the room lifts in clouds.

That night at home my mother and father are in bed and the crack of light under their door has expired. I am in my bed.

It is a warm night. A summer night.

My legs ache. They ache with growing and they ache deep down inside. It is bone ache. I push the covers back from my body and pull up my nightwear. I look at my legs.

At first I think it must be the lamp: it is a harsh shadeless bulb, and tends to distort.

I take a closer look.

And then I see.

My legs are made of glass.

I know they are because I can see through the skin, the surface. I can see the veins and the arteries.

Busy, busy, red and blue blood. I see the outline of muscles.

I am one of the illustrations we have on the walls of the biology room.

I cover myself up. What to do? What to do?

Perhaps it was a trick of the mind. I uncover myself. No. No. My legs are made of glass.

The next morning I don't get out of bed. I daren't.

If I do, I know what will happen. They will shatter. For this is not bulletproof shatterproof reinforced glass. This is molten sand, translucent substance, as old as the first window.

I am made of an ancient material.

I am fragile.

My mother comes upstairs and sees that I am still in bed.

– Are you ill? she asks.

I shake my head. For I am not ill; I am just shocked.

– Eve, she says, – speak to me.

But I say nothing for how do I explain?

She calls my father and he runs quickly up the stairs, in response to the note of alarm in her voice. They stand in the doorway. They stare at me. My mother moves first. She walks towards the bed. – Let me help you.

I shake my head gently. If I shake it too hard I know I will break my neck. She comes closer. I have to say something. – Don't touch me.

My voice is fragile, has the tone of a finger flicking glass.

I lift my arm. Translucent. Beneath the glass I see veins and bone and muscle. I am a walking model of a human being. I am a demonstration of how the body works. There are no secrets.

– Look, I say.

She looks at my arm. – I don't know what I should be looking at.

– This. It's made of glass. I am made of glass.

My mother turns to my father. – What can she mean?

My father is silent.

My mother sinks to her knees by my bedside. – You aren't made of glass, she says. – What is wrong with you to think this of yourself?

She reaches out to hold my hand. I gasp. – If you touch me, I say, – I will break.

My father approaches. They stand together and look down upon me.

– Nothing has changed, my father says.

– Oh, you are so wrong, I say. – Everything has changed.

They leave me on my own so that I can spend a day in bed and realise that there is nothing wrong with me.

When they close the door I am relieved.

I place both arms under the covers as I do not want to see what is inside my body.

I lie, still.

A long time passes then I hear footsteps, and the door opens. A plate of food is placed by my bed and a glass of water. I do not touch them: they revolt me.

I do not read. This is the first day I have not consumed any words.

I try to imagine going to school. The corridors would be busy and full of people carrying bags. They would collide into me. Pieces of me would break off.

I look at the glass of water. Turn my face to the wall.

My mother returns in the afternoon. She sees the full glass, sees the wasted food.

She cries. – You have to eat.

She puts down a plate with a peeled and sliced apple.

I am not tempted.

I am left alone again. The sun has drifted westwards and each corner of the room is gathering dark.

It is a warm night. A summer night.

The books are closed. The books are too heavy to lift.

The lids of my eyes are heavy. They must be for they are made of glass. They are brittle. I must close them for they are heavy and I do not think I can keep them open.

When I wake I look at the window. The leaves have slipped from the trees. The windowsill outside my room is white. It is thick with snow. My breath emerges from my mouth in clouds.

I have lost time.

I lift a hand: glass glass glass.

I did not dream it.

I hear something in the room. Slight click of knees, air exhaled as a body adjusts itself, the creak of a chair. Then silence.

I don't look.

I won't.

I look at the white landscape of the wall, look up at the ceiling, the land of crack and cobweb.

My mind is active: thrum thrum. My skull is warm with thoughts.

There is a movement from the chair. I turn my head towards the centre of the room.

And I see him.

His hair has been cut. I can see his two eyes. They are so pale, so large and pale, that the pupils are specks of dirt.

– What are you doing here? I ask.

My voice is fragile, has the tone of a finger flicking glass, has the tone of a wet finger run round the top of a glass. Has the tone of a glass girl.

– You've been asleep for a long time, he says.

– I know.

I pull the covers up to my chin in case he can see my glass skin.

– I don't want you here, I say.

He shrugs, the only movement in the room. – What you want doesn't interest me.

He is sitting, has a stillness which is uncommon. His hands sit in his lap, obedient.

– Do you know what has happened to me? I ask.

He nods. – You have turned into a girl made of glass.

I stare at him.

– It is true, isn't it?

– It's what you say. Therefore it's true.

We stay like that for a while: I am under the covers; he sits.

He speaks:

– Your mother says you aren't eating.

I feel myself under the covers. Sharp edges, cool smooth surfaces. I am empty.

– Your mother says you won't drink.

He brings out a stone flask, a flagon. He pulls out a wide cork, pours the contents into a glass. – I brought you this.

I look at it.

It is liquid tinged green with small floating particles.

– It's from the river, he says.

He stands, lifts the water and holds it to my lips. I hear the glass hit my glass lip, hear it clink. I shrink backwards into the pillow.

– You'll break me, I say.

– I won't. Drink.

He tips the glass and the first drops go onto my lips, into my mouth. I can taste the bed of the river, the gravel and the weed. I can taste the skin of a trout.

He waits until I have drunk as much as I can and then takes the glass away. He places it on the table.

Fresh snow has begun to fall against the window. It lands in silent slumps. My breath is clouded.

Dark comes.

I ask if he is going home but he says nothing. His eyes are closed. He sleeps.

I pull down the covers and pull up my nightclothes. I see my glass legs.

I pull my clothes up further, see my glass pelvis, the hip bones. I see through my belly into the cavity, see the cave womb and the unfurled bracken stalks which hold my eggs.

The night comes but sleep doesn't.

The moon has risen and its light has entered the room.

I whisper. – Are you awake?

– Yes.

– You were staring at me, I say.

– I know.

– I am not an exhibit.

He smiles. – There aren't many girls made of glass.

The moon-silvered room makes me bold. Words come easily, like water.

– There is nothing to see, I say.

He thinks for a moment. – Because you are transparent?

– Yes.

– But I can see you, he says.

– O.

– You are not transparent to me. And you are not transparent to everyone who has wanted to come and see you.

– They want to see me?

– Yes. Your father has had to turn them away.

– O.

– By being made of glass you are attracting attention.

– O, I say. – I see. But I don't want attention.

He shrugs. – You have to expect it.

I lie and think. My skull is warm with thoughts; each tightly knitted-together tectonic plate thrums with thoughts.

– Do I appear of coloured glass? I ask. – Is that why I am not transparent to you?

– Coloured glass? he says. – No.

– Then, I say, – if I am not clear glass and not coloured glass, are you saying I'm not made of glass?

– I am just saying how you appear to me. Nothing more than that.

– O.

The room is cold and yet he sits there. The snow piles up against the window flake upon flake. It is as though it wants to come in, to escape the cold. The moon reflects off the snow and illuminates the room. It is a cold clear blue.

The river water in the glass by the bed has iced over.

His arms are wrapped around his own self. He blows his hands, rubs them together.

– You are cold, I say.

– Yes. I am cold.

– You need to get warm, I say.

– Yes.

He does need to get warm. If he remains like this, sitting here all night, his blood will freeze in his veins. But what to do? What to do?

I lift the corner of the covers, look at my glass body. Moon and snow and light glint off me.

I am too cold. I will chill him to the bone. I put the covers down.

He is looking at me. I can see the pale blue of his eyes; they are the colour of the snow at the window with the moon through it.

He stands up from his chair. Takes the three steps towards me. My hands are under the covers. My hands are together as if in prayer.

He touches my face with his cold fingers. I am scared I will make him colder, but he takes the covers in his other hand and lifts them up. He gets into the bed beside me. He lies next to me.

We do not touch.

We both look up at the ceiling. We are lit cold blue.

After a few minutes he moves towards me. I feel his warm skin.

I imagine how I must feel to him: smooth, cool, unyielding.

– Do I feel cold? I ask.

– No.

– O.

– You feel warm.

We lie under the covers and the wind outside starts to blow. Snow drifts onto the window.

I feel him by my side. He holds me.

The wind builds. Blows.

The snow starts to smash against the window, it batters. The flakes are heavy. There is the sound of cracking then the glass of the window splinters and breaks.

The snow enters, falls on the bed, the floor, the chair.

Through all this we hold each other.

By dawn it has stopped.

I open my eyes. We lie under a blanket under a blanket of snow. The sun reflects off each flake: light fills the room.

His eyes are closed. He sleeps.

I am warm under the covers. His skin touches mine and he is warm.

It is time to look. I lift the covers carefully so that the snow doesn't fall into the bed. I look first at his body. His skin is pale and I watch his chest rise and fall with each breath.

It is time to look. I lift the covers further until I can see myself. My nightclothes have gone and I see my naked self.

I see veins and bones and muscles.

But then, while I am looking, something happens. I see that my legs and arms slowly begin to cloud over. I hold up my hand: I watch as my glass skin becomes opaque, each finger in turn.

I look down at my cave womb and my glass pelvis.

They too cloud over and become white, as though they are being filled with milk. The unfurled stalks which hold my eggs have gone.

The last to change is my breasts. When they are done I am pale and I am covered in specks of brown, like mud flicked up after the plough.

I place the cover back down and wait for him to wake.

OPENING WINDOWS

Marcos Giralt Torrente
translated by Samantha Schnee

Things weren't turning out as planned. In the morning I had whiled away the hours in front of the computer without managing to write so much as two sentences with any conviction. Elena, my teenage daughter, came into my studio when I had already given up.

'What are you doing?'

I had to admit it, there was nothing else to say: 'Thinking.'

Elena received the MC1R gene from both sides of the family, which means she's a redhead. Not many people know that redheads have some other unusual characteristics, apart from their hair colour, freckles and pale skin. They're more sensitive to changes in temperature and they need more anaesthesia than other people. It's also unusual for them to have blue eyes. So unusual that the ones like Elena who do are believed to bring good luck in Nordic cultures. Perhaps that's why she's always thought of herself as special. Unlike me, she never gives up. Her self-confidence is enviable and I'd even say she's stubborn, though she's also childish and would never intentionally cause offence. She gets angry, of course, but she doesn't get irony.

'I ate. I'm going out.'

Two bullets, two sentences delivered so quickly that it would have been awkward to ask her for a kiss or where she was headed. When she was little she'd ask me how my writing was going, and her eyes shone with pride when she talked about my work. Now, when I catch her looking at me, it feels like none of my secrets escape her scrutiny.

Elena's mother used to say we shouldn't count on her nymph-like invincibility, that her sharp awareness of her extraordinariness was the source of her strength but also her main weakness, and that people like her don't handle crises well. I try not to forget that.

Two or three hours later I was chatting with our neighbour, the one I sometimes accompany on walks with his dog, about everything and nothing.

The position of an outsider in a small town is permanent, and, as we slowly learned, the phases are similar for everyone: the period of arrival, during which we got to know the place, the period when we tried to become accepted, and the period of disillusionment. And disgruntled outsiders generally attract disgruntled locals, who feed their discontent, which would have been the case with Claudio if it weren't for the fact that my disillusionment was more internal than external, and his painstaking deconstructions of each admirable feature of our surroundings went in one ear and out the other due to my deep malaise. I wasn't truly living life there, but then I didn't really know where else I would.

We were walking home. It was the summer that Islamic State began decapitating hostages in the desert, but Claudio and I were both at an age when everything that happens seems to be a mundane repetition of the vicissitudes of life and the shock hardly registered on us. Claudio had been living with his brother's wife and son for a few months. A situation I imagined was difficult, one he didn't talk about and that I didn't broach. Ever since I had started to join him on his walks we met up after supper and, depending on our mood, we'd either walk up the mountain or take the path to the lighthouse. That day we opted for the former, which was long, so we left a few hours earlier than usual: it was the feast of St Samuel, the town's patron saint, and it would have been rude to arrive late at the festivities, which, this year, included a culinary competition and a play put on by some of the students from Elena's school, in addition to the usual musical performance.

'A lot of people will have an eye out for your daughter tonight.'

Claudio didn't seem to like Elena very much. Outside his home, forbidden territory I couldn't even begin to hypothesise about, he gave the impression of a self-made man: naturally intolerant when it came to juvenile behaviour that might seem weak or excessive.

'Why do you say that?'

'Right now she and three other kids are the talk of the town.'

Although no one had put it quite that way, he wasn't the first to bring it up. Elena had developed a crush on a boy who wasn't a good match for her, besides which he was in love with her best friend, who, after a brief courtship, had dumped him for someone else. If the story had been like one of the screenplays I used to write for television, it would have had only two possible outcomes, depending on whether it was a drama or a comedy. Fortunately, life's not that simple. The only thing that was worrying me was Elena's stubbornness, which made her vulnerable, and I suppose that's what Claudio was trying to warn me about.

'Do you know something I should know?'

'Not yet.'

The festival was taking place in the field next to the chapel. They had a stage and two drinks stands with wooden tables where they were serving cold meats and cheese. Maria, the pharmacist, glanced at me from one of them. Two years earlier, shortly after I arrived, we had slept together a few times and now she was the only person in town who had something against me. Her husband looked at me, too, and smiled inscrutably.

I wondered what I would have done in his shoes. I had plenty of experience when it came to adultery, but so far as I knew, only from one perspective. Oscar Wilde wrote, 'When one is in love, one always begins by deceiving one's self, and one always ends by deceiving others'. It would make more sense to reverse the two as far as I'm concerned.

'How thoughtful, you've dressed for the occasion,' Claudio, who was wearing the same windbreaker and muddy jeans he'd worn on our walk, exclaimed.

'You know I'm not at liberty to do whatever I want like you. I'm watched much more carefully.'

I had changed my trousers and my shoes, and donned the light wool jacket that Elena's mother called my summer uniform. We bought it together, back when we first met, on a trip to London, and I had worn it thousands of times with her. When she died I moved it to the back of my closet. It's strange how the same objects we avoid when we're grieving because of the painful memories they bring back become stimuli for our memories once grieving has ended.

'Have you seen Elena?' I asked.

'No,' Claudio said. 'But I'm under orders to find my nephew for his mother, and it's no bother to include her in my search. You want me to tell her anything if I do?'

'Just let me know if you see her.'

'At your command.'

He immediately turned away, with a flourish, and disappeared into the crowd that was gathering in response to the mayor's announcement from the stage. As he walked away I pondered the barriers we erect to preserve our privacy. I had friends I hadn't seen for years, and with whom it would be difficult to recover our former intimacy, but who nevertheless were permanent fixtures in my life, more so than recent friends like Claudio, who would never be more than passing acquaintances. And the same could possibly be said about lots of other things. We often cling to our past selves, not allowing new things a fair chance. Which goals replace outdated ones? What ideals do we keep when we discard old ones? When you look at it this way, the passage of time is terrifying, because, as we gradually let go of our baggage, we grow further and further from ourselves. A terrible lesson for our children, who ought to know their parents at the height of their powers, not in defeat. Children ought to be able to believe that illusions aren't fleeting, that we can be counted on no matter what, even when our enthusiasm for life begins to flag.

After his welcome speech, the mayor called the judges of the culinary competition to the stage and blindfolded them to prepare for the competition. The competitors followed. One of them was the pharmacist, who tripped on the last step and nearly dropped her dish. Why did I choose her and not someone else? Apart from the fact that she seemed unlikely to turn me down, there was no apparent reason. What a selfish game seduction is; once consummated, attraction dies, leaving in its wake a dearth of morality and feeble intentions to make amends. I was going to get a drink when I saw Elena passing right by me. I hurried over, just managing to grab her shoulder.

'What?' she asked. She sounded annoyed, she kept glancing around. She furrowed her brow and for a moment her orange eyebrows moved closer together.

'Don't you want to spend some time with me?'

When she was little I was constantly afraid of dying prematurely and leaving her behind. It never occurred to me that I might be the one left alone to care for her.

'Not now, Dad. They're waiting for me.'

Elena shrugged my hand off her shoulder and took a step back as if to make her point. She had been wearing makeup and nail polish for a while now. What did mothers do with their daughters? Did they have the nerve to tell them not to use too much? Did they advise them not to chase boys? Did they forbid it if the boy in question was interested in someone else?

'All right. But don't forget about me.'

Before I knew what was happening she leaned in and kissed me.

'Don't be silly. Of course I won't forget you.'

I had tried to give her a knowing wink and the results exceeded my expectations. Then she slipped away, as if this show of affection was her final penance for regaining her freedom, and all I could see was her back receding from me. Her gait was like her mother's, loose and energetic. I would have given almost anything for her to get what she wanted. If it really was this boy, then that was fine. My only child didn't deserve to suffer unnecessarily. A few months earlier, on the second anniversary of her mother's death, I had asked Elena if she missed her. The answer she gave was both reassuring and disturbing.

'Mum's not dead,' she said. 'She's inside me.'

Ever since she was little Elena had often witnessed arguments between her mother and me that she never should have seen. With careless disregard, we involved her in each crisis. She had seen me storm out of the house and not return for days, she had heard her mother accusing me of infidelities and many other things – with or without reason – to wound me in return. The consequences were disturbing. When she was five years old she used to give us a daily medical report on an imaginary friend who suffered for months on end. When she was eight she put us into a state of apprehension when we found her parakeet's cage open and empty, with no explanation. Later, things got better. Our separation, which seemed inevitable, never happened. Love prevented it, but though that love was greater than the obstacles her mother and I had created, it was impossible to express as strongly as we had expressed our doubts about it. For those who don't experience love's ups and downs, time substantiates love, but we didn't have enough. You could say it's a miracle that Elena didn't harbour any resentment. We had exposed her to too many things beyond her ken. Had she understood? The truth was elusive, a confusion of mixed signals.

Meanwhile, Elena had gone over to the edge of the field where the festivities were taking place, her red head fading into the shadows of a group of kids who were waiting for the concert to start; the competition judges were deliberating and I had sidled up to one of the bars.

'It's great to see you two together. You look like you get on well.'

It was Claudio's sister-in-law talking to me. I had ordered a beer without recognising her, because her hair was pulled back in a hairnet. Our interactions, as my slip proved, had been scarce. Until her husband died she had lived with him and their son in her hometown, and we hadn't seen much of each other ever since she had come to live with Claudio for obscure financial reasons.

'Thanks.'

'Has Claudio told you that I'd like you to talk to Amleto?'

Amleto was the name of her son. Apparently she and her husband had spent their honeymoon in Rome and returned with this unlikely gift for their future offspring.

'Yes,' I lied.

'He spends all his money on books. He's very sensitive. I think getting to know a real writer would be good for him.'

There the accusation was again: *writer*. Not a day passed without someone uttering the word. A reminder, pronounced with the best of intentions, which should have flattered me.

'Tell him to come over to my place.'

I didn't protest. Since I was going through a dry spell I was well aware that almost everything I was proud of, except for Elena, I owed to writing. The excuses I made to try to justify my meagre output simply didn't work anymore, I had tried them all. And on top of that I felt like I had acted selfishly in my attempt to find a solution. I mean our departure from the city, which I had undertaken thinking more of myself than of Elena.

'I'll tell him, though he probably won't have the nerve. It would be better if you and your daughter came over to our place. I don't understand why she and Amleto haven't made friends with each other.'

My daughter doesn't like orphans. My daughter is in the forest now, chasing a farm-boy who's not interested in her. My daughter is an extraordinary, obstinate girl who prefers to extinguish one grief with another, and I should take her far away from here and provide her with something better than I'm providing her with now. I thought all this exactly as I have written it, but I didn't say it. Instead, I suggested a date for us to come to their house and then I picked up my beer and, once I was certain that the pharmacist had been eliminated and that the competition was down to two finalists, I walked away, feigning interest in what was happening on stage. Just as I was walking away I ran into Claudio, who was coming from the opposite direction.

'Elena's down by the spring,' he said. 'It's teenage mayhem over there. You can't move without bumping into a couple. But don't worry about her. She's part of a threesome.'

'Are you village folk always so funny?'

'I'm serious,' he replied. 'It looks to me like there's been an unexpected change in affinities that favours her interests. The main Don Juan seems to be vacillating between the two young ladies and the other guy's the desperate one now. But don't get too excited.'

Claudio smiled and I responded by taking a sip of my beer. Though I was grateful for the information, part of me felt sheepish and depressed. Despite the fact that I relied on true stories for my writing, I had avoided the subject of other people's personal affairs ever since my marriage had nearly broken up thanks to wagging tongues. Fear of gossip had also influenced my decision to break off my brief affair with the pharmacist: I certainly didn't want Elena to find out. I suppose it made no difference. Claudio wasn't dangerous that way, but his glibness bothered me, especially in contrast to his silence about his own affairs.

'I got lucky with Elena, but I still haven't found my nephew,' Claudio added. 'I'm going to tell his mother, I'll be right back.'

'I was just with her. I didn't know she was working the drinks stand.'

'Oh, yeah, right,' he stammered. 'You know, she's doing what she can to become accepted in town.'

This time Claudio didn't wait for my response, a sign that he had said too much for his own liking. He walked away in a hurry and I continued on my way to the raised area in front of the stage. They had just announced the ecstatic winner of the competition and the mayor had the mike again, he was telling people to be patient. He reminded them that before the concert, there was going to be a short theatre piece put on by some of the kids in town.

'Boring!' someone next to me shouted.

'Yeah, boring!' other voices echoed.

Despite the apparent lack of enthusiasm, many people who had finished eating began to politely leave the wooden tables and take up positions in front of the makeshift stage, where the mayor had moved out of the way of two kids busy preparing a rudimentary set: a sofa suite, a lamp . . . Other kids were coming over from the remote area where Elena had gone, joining the audience in small groups. A swarm of moths had gathered around one of the streetlamps, colliding with the bulb. Claudio was still at the drinks stand his sister-in-law was tending. There was an air of expectation, curiosity even, which was creating an excited buzz. Nevertheless, most people in the audience didn't seem to notice when the novice stage-hands left the stage and, after a brief pause, the first scene commenced: a young man playing the part of a child lay on the carpet, playing with an aeroplane, while a couple his age, perhaps his parents, cuddled on the sofa nearby.

'Tell me you love me, tell me it's not over.'

'What should we do? We've got to make a decision.'

'Shit! What's Amleto doing up there?' Claudio asked. He had sidled up to me without my realising it, and he offered me a beer and paper plate of cured ham.

I had caught a glimpse of Elena's red hair moving through the audience and for a few seconds I was pre-occupied trying to figure out whether she was going to stay for the play or leave again, so I hadn't noticed that Claudio's nephew had taken the stage and was waiting in the corner. The way he held himself left no doubt that he was part of the play.

'You didn't know?' I asked, while I stooped over to put my beer bottle on the ground.

Claudio hesitated to reply.

'His mother has noticed he's been out more than usual lately.'

'He probably wanted to surprise you,' I said, stating the obvious, not the most appropriate thing to say, just the first thing that came to mind. Through a gap in the crowd I saw Elena had found a place to watch with her friends, three or four rows in front of me, and she was standing next to the boy she liked.

The sound of awkward footsteps boomed through the loudspeaker.

'Hurry! You have to leave.'

The couple on the sofa had jumped up and run to the side of the stage, where the woman pretended to lift a sash window through which the man escaped just before another actor pretended to open a door and burst into the room. What had seemed like a peaceful family scene had become a crude depiction of adultery. To complete the cliché, the woman ran over to greet the new arrival, who yielded to her contentedly, unaware of what he had interrupted.

'Sit down, put your feet up. I'll make dinner for you.'

'And the boy?' Claudio asked sarcastically, engrossed in the play. 'Everyone has forgotten the boy.'

It wasn't a trivial observation. The mother paid exaggerated attention to the man who was apparently her husband, looking periodically at the window through which her lover had escaped, while the boy continued playing with the toy plane, wrapped up in his own world; it was difficult to tell whether his absorption was part of the staging or if the actor had forgotten his lines. It became clear it was the former when Amleto's character took a step closer to centre stage without speaking. At that point the actor who was playing the boy stood up, abandoning his childish pose, while the actor who was playing the father lay down on the floor like a corpse while the wife/mother pretended to cry, a shawl wrapped around her to symbolise the passage of time.

No one was watching the play apart from us and a few other people, including Elena. There were probably some busybodies in the crowd who would make it their business to remind people in town about the play later, but at that moment it seemed like no one was paying attention. There were groups of teens eating sunflower seeds and groups of adults talking, as well as singletons who were wandering around, pausing with one group and then another. I told Claudio that the kid looked like he had grown, but he didn't reply; his sarcasm had failed him, he was lost for words. I guessed it wouldn't be long before the lover reappeared, and I was right, of course. The corpse had gotten up and walked away, and only the mother and son remained onstage. The way he returned to the stage dramatised a leap into the future: he opened the door with his key, repeating the dead husband's movements. Claudio didn't say a word, the world had gone quiet, even Elena wasn't talking. She didn't look around for me and her movements, as observed from a distance, didn't reveal any uneasiness. And then, the moment we had all been waiting for: Amleto's soliloquy. He walked slowly to the centre of the stage, grabbed a chair, and sat down facing the audience leaning against the chair back.

'Mother, I remember everything. About you and me. You should never have made me your accomplice. Was it really necessary? I'd still know what I know now, but I'd have different memories. How do you think he felt? Were all those years of secrecy – when I saw and heard everything – really for me? What I'm about to say isn't rehearsed. No one has

*taken advantage of us, we haven't been misused. I've had
milk and cereal for breakfast every morning and there was
someone waiting at the school gates for me every afternoon.
I realised I was growing a moustache two winters ago. I've
shaved ever since, with scissors at first, and with a razor for a
while now. The thing is, I can't remember the day Dad laughed
when he saw me with the scissors without remembering that
same day I was keeping him busy while you were saying your
goodbyes in the sunroom. The next morning you could still see
the footprints in the rose bed. But no matter: someone raked
the earth a few days later. Very few things stay the same.
What matters to us today won't matter to us tomorrow. I
have an idea of how I'll remember him thirty years from now.
Distantly. Nevertheless, it's impossible to obliterate memory.
That is your crime.'*

Amleto stressed the last sentence and fell silent. It
was a rhetorical silence. He was immobile, but his wide
eyes spoke volumes. The mayor had returned to the
podium and was waiting for him to finish. Curious, I
looked at Claudio, who was standing on tiptoe, like he
was trying to get a better view of the drinks stand. He
looked right past me, it was impossible to tell whether
he was avoiding my gaze or whether he was oblivious.
Elena's romance was progressing. The other couple had
slipped away and left her alone with the boy. What matters to us today won't necessarily matter to us tomorrow.
Tomorrow brings worries that supersede yesterday's. I
wasn't entirely sure that was true, but it made more

sense to believe this theory, though imperfect, than to risk losing what's good about the present.

Someone in the audience shouted, 'Start the music!' and other voices chimed in. Amleto had gotten out of the chair as slowly as he had taken the stage. Standing there, with his hands in his pockets, he launched into the end of his soliloquy.

'Mother, I don't have much experience. I don't know what can be done about wrongs once they've been committed, I suppose sometimes the only solution is to wrap them all in a bundle and throw them in the river. You've done the opposite. You've built a monument, and you've kept yourself afloat by hanging on to it, diminishing the space between us without realising that there's no room left for mystery or joy. In doing so, you've kept alive what you wanted to erase, on top of which you've been unfair to the one you love. You thought that, just by sharing a bed, you were sharing everything. Mother, we're running out of time. Stop putting pressure on me, and set all three of us free. Don't make me save myself, don't force me to assuage your guilt with mine.'

Amleto glanced enigmatically at the audience, turned around, and stepped off the platform.

'I couldn't hear. What did he say?' Claudio asked me.

The mayor was calling for applause for the actors.

'She shouldn't force him to assuage her guilt with his.'

'Whose?'

I thought about saying 'his mother's' but without thinking I gave into impulse. Amleto was back onstage, holding hands with the rest of the cast. Elena was clapping, clapping and whistling. I wanted to see her face, to read her expression. When all was said and done, perhaps it was possible to live they way she wanted to, light-heartedly.

'Your sister-in-law's,' I murmured.

Although Claudio was immediately taken aback by my boldness, his expression was one of surprise, not offence. He paused, as if he were deciding what to say in reply, but he changed the subject.

'What are you going to do?' he asked. 'Are you staying for the concert?'

'A while,' I replied. 'You?'

'I don't know. I think I'll go home.'

Elena wasn't clapping anymore and her friend took advantage of the moment to steal a kiss from her. They laughed. Then Elena took his hand and they began to leave. Claudio had given me a second chance, and I didn't pass it up.

'Don't you think you should go to her?' I asked, lifting my chin in the direction of the drinks stand his sister-in-law was tending. The musicians were busy tuning their instruments, Elena and the boy were walking against the flow of people responding to the first strains of the music. In less than a minute they'd pass right by us, if they didn't change their path. What you do in one minute, what you decide and what you say, can last forever. To behave as if we have this time at our disposal only to be judged is perhaps the best service we can afford the people who surround us, and ourselves.

'You're right,' Claudio replied, unexpectedly.

I moved my tongue in my mouth, I puffed out my cheeks, I stretched the muscles of my face, I smiled. Elena had seen me, and instead of hurrying away, she was walking towards me, unembarrassed to be holding hands. To watch a child grow up is to witness life in motion. Stepping away from life to write about it is the curious paradox that writers experience. You have to open the windows and let life in. Not just because the spectacle is well worth it: without changing water and sap and air and blood into ink it's difficult to create something truly worthwhile.

'Though I'm tempted to go find my nephew first,' Claudio added with a touch of irony. 'Calling himself Amleto and having the nerve to put on such an absurdity – he deserves a real talking to.'

'I liked it,' Elena, who had finally reached us, said emphatically.

The orchestra was ready, the singer was making the obligatory opening remarks while the musicians quietly played the first tune of the night; a sudden whiff of humidity, like that of a storm, blew in on the wind from the mountain.

'It's not that I didn't like it, it's because of his name,' Claudio responded, without managing to explain any further.

Despite the obvious joy she felt in the company of her friend, Elena looked at Claudio with irritation, he was tongue-tied and I wanted to help him out.

'Amleto is the Italian name for the most famous prince of Denmark.'

Elena's eyes, two blue lanterns in a forest of flame, paused for a few seconds to digest this information. Behind her, latecomers of all ages were running to the bars to get drinks.

'Who was also foolish enough to put on a play for his mother and his uncle, of course.'

If Claudio felt the unintentional blow in *also*, he didn't show it. After pronouncing these words I kissed Elena, grabbed the paper plate with the ham, which was practically untouched, as was the bottle of beer that Claudio was holding – he had been frozen in that pose since he had arrived – and I leaned over to pick up mine.

'All right, everybody, go about your business,' I said when I stood up. Since no one moved, I smiled animatedly by way of a goodbye and walked off in search of the rubbish bin. The stars were hidden by thick cloud cover but it didn't seem like it was going to rain. For the second time that night I had the sense that Elena's mother wasn't very far away and I felt at peace.

THE PIANO BAR

Hisham Matar

I was in a state of unease when one evening I found myself wandering into the Piano Bar. The windowless room is the only public establishment I know of in Cairo where one could go largely unnoticed. It is so faintly lit that on first entering you could hardly make out whether anyone was sitting in the low leather armchairs arranged in clusters around coffee tables along the edges. Only in the centre of the room, where a large hexagonal bar stood, did a light burn above the waiter's head. Around him a deep maple counter gleamed warmly. The same maple also panelled the walls, the blond pushing through the varnish whenever one of the patrons there struck a match. It stopped just above head-height, where wall-paper, with the pattern of a grotesquely enlarged and mutating vermilion thistle, climbed all the way up to the extraordinarily high ceiling. The room was at least as high as it was wide.

I had discovered the bar accidentally. I was due to attend a dinner party at the home of a couple I hardly knew. The invitation had arrived by telephone a fortnight earlier. It seemed so far in advance then that I immediately accepted. I even felt excited at the prospect. But as the date approached my doubts increased. On the morning of the party I could do little besides oscillate between going and cancelling, coming up with several credible excuses. By the afternoon, when it was too late to pull out, unless the excuse was dramatic, such as a sudden fever or a car crash, I resigned myself to attending the dinner. Buttoning on a fresh shirt, I heard myself speak the mantra that was turning in my head, 'It will be fine, it will be fine,' sounding like my father, bringing to mind one of the labels he had given me: 'An Indoor Child'. I blamed my reticence, and still do, on Cairo, the city that won't rest until each one of its inhabitants is dispossessed of his privacy. In fact, even in bed in my darkened room I can feel its presence: reproachful, inquisitive, and utterly relentless. And yet, here I am; I have returned home to my country after many years abroad, and after my parents have left. I have moved back but remain in the same situation as before: to see my mother and father, I must board a plane.

One needs to build new bridges.

I was glad I had implicated myself into attending the dinner. The question that remained was what to bring. Flowers could stand the risk of either being taken for an effeminate gift or, if the husband was one of those men who were constantly on guard, a covert sign of flirtation with the lady. A cake was predictable but safe. I went to the bakery in the Marriott Hotel, a large modern compound that had swallowed up one of the palaces of the now long-deposed King Farouk. Wanting to be sur-rounded by fine old objects, I quickly walked through a couple of the palace rooms, carrying the cake from its yellow ribbon in one hand. I knew the hotel well. In all the years I was away, wanting to remain in contact with my parents but not be folded into the urgencies of their lives, I would stay here on my brief but frequent visits to Cairo. But I had never noticed the Piano Bar before, tucked away as it is down one end of a narrow, marbled corridor. I thought of fetching the book from my car, Thomas Shelton's 1612 English translation of *Don Quixote*, and reading it in the bar whilst tucking into the cake. The picture was amusing.

The dinner party was a bland affair. There were several heroic but futile attempts by the hosts and their guests to raise the tempo. Every so often one of them would announce an incendiary conclusion – 'A real revolution will only guarantee democracy by eradicating the elite', 'Democracy will never work in Egypt', or 'The only way to govern this country is with a whip'. I had successfully avoided all the pitfalls whilst not seeming altogether disinterested. There was only one moment of danger, when I was asked a direct question and had to pretend to be thinking. Then, as often happens when one hesitates, someone stepped in and spoke on my behalf: 'Let me tell you what Khaled is thinking . . . '

When it was appropriate to leave, I walked out feeling agitated. Instead of going directly to my apartment, I drove back to the hotel, parked, pulled out the book from the glove compartment and walked in a straight line to the Piano Bar. This time I could see that the room was not entirely unfamiliar, which had probably accounted, at least in part, for its appeal. One of the framed photographs in Father's study was taken here. In it he is a young man, standing stiffly beside King Farouk, the Egyptian king's arm is wrapped around Father's shoulders. This used to be the king's games room. When the royal palace was converted into a hotel, the snooker table was removed and a bar was built in its place. A grand piano now stood awkwardly in one corner. It was the thistle wallpaper, which even through the old black-and-white photograph was unforgettable, that allowed me to make the connection. The same old crystal chandelier remained and now hung too low above the bar. It looked like a huge spider captured by an electric current.

The waiter behind the bar, dressed in an azure shirt and dark blue waistcoat, wore no necktie. His collar was open by two buttons. A yellow carnation, the edges of each petal stained crimson, was plunged into the lapel of his waistcoat. He saw me approach. For some reason, I hesitated. I placed the book on the bar and looked at the time. I dug a hand in one trouser pocket, the other in my jacket pocket, then placed a finger where a breast pocket would have been had the shirt I was wearing that evening had one. Suddenly I could not wait to be out of the dim opulence. Although I could not yet see the faces of those sitting and speaking in low voices in the periphery, I suspected that they had their eyes on me. As often happens, my embarrassment turned into annoyance and so when I looked in their direction I looked harshly. That was when I spotted a man walking into the bar. He descended with great effort into one of the low armchairs. I thought I recognised him. I took my book and walked towards him. I was almost certain.

'Ustaz Hosam?' I asked. 'Hosam Gafar?'

'Who?' the man said, still undecided which way to stretch his legs.

Hosam Gafar had once worked for my father. He ran his office in Cairo.

'Do you recall who I am?' I said.

'Who?' he said again.

Another man came towards us and stood facing me. I immediately became defensive and stuttered the word 'I'.

'Sir,' the man I thought was Hosam Gafar said. 'I am sorry but I am not sure who you are. What do you want?'

'I'm Khaled, Khaled Gamish. Ali Gamish's son.'

Hearing my father's name returned to me an old confidence.

'By God,' Hosam Gafar said, standing.

He peered into my face. He pulled me under the light of the bar to see properly. I wondered what the other patrons were making of this.

'By God, it is Ali Pasha's son,' he said, and embraced me so quickly that I did not have time to open my arms. My hands and that fat volume of Shelton's *Don Quixote* were awkwardly sandwiched between us. 'What's this,' Hosam said, looking at the book. 'Are you studying?' And before I could respond he waved to his companion to come.

I caught the waiter smiling to himself.

The other man came and was no longer suspicious but imploring me to join them. I agreed. I passed the book from one hand to the other, searched my pockets again.

'Have you misplaced something?' Hosam asked.

'No,' I said, then waved my hand as if dismissing an insignificant detail.

We sat in a triangle with the round coffee table between us. The back and sides of the armchair were so fatly padded that the seat held me tightly. I placed the book on my lap and was glad Hosam did not repeat his question about whether I was studying.

'How are you, Khaled Bey?' he asked and then, before I could answer, introduced his friend. 'Mustafa Khalaf, an old friend, a man I trust implicitly.'

'It is neither here nor there whether you trust him or if that trust is implicit for I have no secrets to divulge.' I heard the words spill out of me as though spoken by another man, and felt a heat fill my cheeks as I said them. Thankfully, they both laughed, albeit a short, uncertain laugh. 'I had no idea I would find you here,' I said.

'Of course, of course,' Hosam said.

'And when I did I thought I should say hello.'

'Absolutely. I am glad you did.'

Every so often one of them would reveal his teeth and I knew then that they were smiling. The waiter was standing beside us.

'What do you think the German would like?' Hosam asked Mustafa.

'Better wait until he arrives,' Mustafa told him, then leaning towards me he explained, 'How can you know what another man would like? Better let him come and choose for himself. Let every man choose for himself, is what I say.'

'A bottle of Jack Daniels,' Hosam told the waiter. 'And listen, your best meze. Don't be a miser. Spoil us.'

The waiter blushed.

Hosam lit a cigarette and for a couple of seconds I could see his face clearly. I felt the usual mixture of horror and pleasure at finding myself in the presence of someone from Father's world. Just before he blew out the match I caught his eyebrows curling with an earnestness that, although fleetingly witnessed, struck me as put on.

'Look, Khaled Bey,' he began, 'your father was a dear man, and when he vanished, twelve years ago now – oh yes, don't think I can ever forget – I had no idea what to think. I have tried to find out. I mean, when your mother . . . '

There was a hint of disdain in the way he said 'your mother' and I suspected he had stopped mid-sentence because he, too, detected the bitterness. He exhaled an astonishing quantity of smoke, which quickly vanished.

'You see, I was reluctant when she asked me to dissolve everything. She offered no explanation. It was very difficult to know what to do. She simply said you all had moved abroad. "But what do you mean?" I said, and demanded to speak to Ali Pasha, but she said that she was acting on the Pasha's instructions. Then she cried. It is impossible to know what to do when a woman cries.'

Mustafa agreed.

'Forgive me, Khaled Bey,' Hosam continued, 'but her whole demeanour was strange, and so I knew – I am not a child – there was something she wasn't telling me. It just didn't seem right; not something Ali Pasha would do. I knew there were powerful people that had him in their sights, but he would never leave without a word, he would never terminate my lifelong service just like that. But I had no way to him, you understand? And the money; well, the money stopped as quickly as someone turning off a faucet, and you can't run a business without liquidity.'

I nodded. I wondered if it seemed as if I were offering forgiveness. I remembered what my father had told me about his decision: 'Our country is like a coconut, hard on the outside, soft on the inside, nearly impossible to penetrate. When an insect finds a pore and enters, it feeds on the milk but then gets too fat to leave. It then has two choices: either keep on drinking or fast and squeeze out again. I decided to fast.'

'What have you been doing since?' I asked Hosam.

'Well, you know, keeping busy, this and that.' He laughed and his friend, the trustworthy Mustafa Khalaf, shook. Hosam cleared his throat and in a deep voice said, 'This is why we are here.'

'We are here on work,' Mustafa said.

'We are meeting a German,' Hosam said. 'What's his name?' he asked Mustafa.

'Mr Huffmyer.'

'Yes, Huff-whatever.'

Mustafa shook for a second time and I realised that this was how he laughed.

'He works for a large air-conditioning firm in Munich,' Hosam went on. 'What to do, Khaled Bey? Must keep busy, keep these old fingers meddling, or else I might forget everything your father taught me.'

By this time my eyes had grown accustomed to the darkness. I began to notice a vulnerable twitch in Hosam's eyes that vanished as soon as he spoke again.

'And you, Khaled Bey? Are you back here now for good?'

'Yes,' I said.

'Wonderful news,' Hosam said.

'Excellent,' Mustafa said. 'Allow me to tell you, sir, that no matter how far one travels, there is no place like home.'

'What a man, what a marvellous man, your father,' Hosam said. 'He inspired great fear and respect. Once,' he said, lowering his voice, 'a woman came into the office. Young, one of those university types. Wearing a tight skirt and holding a short stack of books against her hip. But she didn't fool me. I suspected she got herself in some trouble and must've thought, 'What the hell, I'll give this a go.' It was always like that, you see: people knew of Ali Pasha's generosity and many came asking for help. You don't need me to tell you,' he said, and this time I nodded too. 'I would advise the Pasha – oh, how many times I told him – "Don't let them take advantage," and he would say, "Be quiet, you stingy bastard."'

Hosam laughed and was joined by his friend who had an astonishing ability of laughing soundlessly. Mustafa slapped the table and the waiter came. Hosam waved him away, but then called him back, a little too loudly. 'Where's our order, man?'

'Right away, sir,' the waiter whispered, perhaps to inspire gentleness in his customer.

'Water at least,' Hosam told him and then returned to telling his story. 'Yes, I swear, he used to do that. If Ali Pasha liked you, he would shout abuse.'

Then, with complete earnestness, Mustafa said, 'It's true; insults can be a sign of affection.'

'Yes,' Hosam said, then emphatically added, 'and the Pasha was like that.'

The waiter returned carrying a large tray.

'Finally!' Hosam told him.

The waiter dealt out the coasters as though they were playing cards. He placed a glass on each and then several small plates of food. He did this with such methodical care and speed that I found pleasure in watching him. Before he could leave, Hosam told him, 'Don't think you can forget about us now.'

'Of course not, sir.'

'Visit us from time to time.'

'And how can I not, sir.'

After the waiter left, Mustafa told Hosam, 'We need another glass.'

'What? Oh yes. Maître?' Hosam called. 'Another glass. We are expecting a guest, a westerner, don't shame us.' And when the waiter returned, Hosam told him, with an authoritative yet affectionate tone, 'Remember to keep these plates full. It would break my heart if I were to see one empty.'

'The German might wish to drink something else,' Mustafa explained, 'but this way, if he fancied whiskey, he could hit the ground running.'

'Yes,' I said.

'Anyway,' Hosam continued, leaning forward. 'About that young woman. She was beautiful. When you watched her from behind, each buttock moved independently.

The Pasha believed that he was better than me; that he could always detect more accurately whether someone was lying. He hated losing.'

'What a lovely man,' Mustafa said.

'Have you met my father?' I asked him.

'No, but Hosam told me so much about him.'

'Mustafa knows everything. Listen, your father didn't mind giving money to a fraudster – even though it used to make my blood boil. What bothered him most was when my intuition proved more accurate than his.'

'And how did you know if someone was lying?' I asked.

'You can always tell,' Hosam said with such certainty that I regretted my question.

'Indeed you can,' Mustafa confirmed.

'Listen, you always know,' Hosam repeated, leaning a little deeper now towards me. 'The sincere ones always look ashamed, whereas the fraudsters, no matter how hard they try, can't stop their eyes glittering when they have your money in their hand. The sons of bitches used to think they were cleverer than us. God will see to them.'

'You can't cheat God,' Mustafa said.

'Oh, how I miss your father,' Hosam said, and I could see that nervous twitch return for a moment. 'And, listen,' he said loudly, looking at Mustafa, 'he almost always won. Incredible talent for seeing through people.'

'Incredible,' Mustafa said, reaching for his drink.

'So this woman walked in.'

'Yes, tell us,' Mustafa said, eagerly.

'She walked in, stabbing both heels into the marble like an army general, putting on kilos and kilos of confidence, speaking in a fancy accent so false it could have been manufactured in China. She stood in front of me and asked for the "Managing Director". I told her, "Listen, mademoiselle, what Managing Director are you talking about?" She said – I still remember her courage, I swear to you, without blushing or even blinking, she said, "*Your* Managing Director." I couldn't help but laugh. I went in to tell the Pasha. I found him standing, tapping the rubber end of a pencil at a place on the globe. He asked me to show her in. I closed the door and left them talking for a long time. They were in there for at least an hour. I couldn't make out what they were saying; I wasn't trying to eavesdrop, of course, but usually you could catch the gist. Halfway through Ali Pasha called the tea boy and asked him to bring a cold glass of water, which usually meant the visitor had become emotional. Suddenly she opened the door and walked out, her heels hardly touching the floor now. When I asked the Pasha he told me, "None of your bloody business," and for years I had no idea what had gone on in there. My mind went to far off places. But then one day I met her on a train to Alexandria. She was dressed all in black. Pretended she didn't know me, but I persisted, reminding her of the day she came to the office, of her interview with *my*

Managing Director. Eventually, she could see I wasn't going to go away . . . '

'Hosam can be persistent,' Mustafa said in praise. 'In fact, he is one of the most persistent people I know. Which is why he is excellent at what he does. I have learnt so much from him. Dogged, in fact. And, as everyone knows, persistence is a virtue.'

'Yes,' I said, 'it is.' Then after a little pause I added, 'That's exactly why I have come back.' These words surprised me. It was an insight arrived at only as I was uttering the words.

Hosam too must have noted it, because he stopped for a moment before continuing. 'Persistence and perseverance,' he said. 'Well, listen, if you don't try, you won't get. Most important of all are your intentions; if you have good intentions, then rest assured God will open roads for you. Anyway, she eventually spoke.'

'But first tell us,' Mustafa interrupted. 'How did you convince her?'

'I was frank. I told her the man she had met was my boss; that I had worked for him for nearly twenty years, ever since I left school; that he had taught me everything I knew and that when a groom asked for my sister's hand Ali Pasha paid for the wedding and bought the newlyweds a fridge-freezer and washing machine, and later, when I got married, he did not allow me to put a hand in my pocket. But then one day this man, under whose shade my entire family sheltered, vanished. I still don't know where or why and so anything of him, the smallest detail, comforts me.'

'You are a decent fellow,' Mustafa said.

'Only the son of a whore would forget,' Hosam said.

'I can see how that won her over,' Mustafa said.

Hosam lit another cigarette and this time the flame illuminated a different face. Tears had welled up in his eyes. For the first time the silence that contained us was not forced. He took out a folded handkerchief and pressed it into each eye.

'Anyway. It turned out her mother had just died. She buried her in Cairo and was now moving to Alexandria. She had an extraordinarily large suitcase, and as heavy as a corpse. I dragged it to the next carriage where there were fewer passengers and we could speak privately. She began telling me of the circumstances that drove her to come asking for help. She was training to be a teacher. Her superior would make the occasional advance when no one was looking. She tried to endure it, but one day he went too far. She decided not to go to the police and that was, of course, her second mistake. The first was not showing him the limit with regards to those advances. Her third was that she agreed to sleep with him once again. "I couldn't forget what happened," she told me, "and thought this might make it right, make it as if it were all my idea." And the man wanted more. And who could blame him? But with every time he became more violent, convinced he could do with her as he pleased.'

'Her fault,' Mustafa said.

'Things got very bad. She didn't know what to say when one day her mother saw the blue ghost of a man's hand around her arm.'

'He needed to be taught a lesson,' Mustafa said.

'If she were my sister I would have killed him,' Hosam told him. 'But also how can you know she was telling the truth? And by that point it was too late.'

'Too late,' Mustafa agreed.

'Now, most of the people who came to the Pasha were what you would expect: a defeated street-sweeper wanting money for medicine for his sick child, one of the porters needing money for school uniforms, that sort of thing. She, on the other hand, was unusual. "How did you know about the Pasha?" I asked her. "I heard from people in the neighbourhood that he was fair and generous," she said. "So what exactly were you expecting him to do? We weren't running a Mafia," I told her. "We weren't going to break the man's legs." "Of course not," she said. "What I asked for was money, a loan, to run away. I thought I could go to Alexandria – I have always loved Alexandria – and teach in a small school where no one knows me." "Where is your family?" the Pasha had asked her, and the woman told him that the only relative she had left was her mother and that she would take the old woman with her. That was when, according to the woman, the Pasha said, "So you want me to pay you to run away and leave the man to do the same to another woman?" The woman didn't know how to respond. Then the Pasha asked her, "Are you otherwise content?" "What do you mean?" she asked him. "In your life," the Pasha said, "and apart from this man, are you otherwise content?" "Yes," she said. "And your mother, is she content also?" "Yes," she said. "Does she want to move to Alexandria?" "No, but I will convince her." "Don't disrupt your life. Old people hate moving. Strengthen your heart. Every time one of us runs the tyrant becomes stronger."' Before a silence could intervene, Hosam said, 'But listen to the wisdom: Every time one of us runs the tyrant becomes stronger.'

'Yes,' Mustafa said, enthusiastically.

Then, to me, Hosam said, 'I told you; Mustafa is an old friend. I have told him all about your father and what happened to him. Don't believe what people say, Khaled Bey. He got too big, is what it was. They came after him because he got too big.'

I was determined not to respond. I looked up towards the high chandelier, which was slightly behind me and to one side. It no longer resembled an electrocuted spider. I could now see elegance in it. Its crystals glittered beautifully. It looked like a blonde woman's hair tied up in a bun. I wondered whether Father's eyes had ever fallen on it during his visits to the palace in order to play snooker with the king, and probably lose to the king, and I wondered also if he had ever observed the resemblance the chandelier paid to a spider and sometimes to a woman's hair. Thinking I needed him, the waiter was coming towards me. Knowing full well that the extravagant chandelier was not a recent addition, I nevertheless asked him, 'Tell me, are the crystals part of the original room?'

'Indeed, sir, the chandelier was certainly part of the original room.'

'The same crystals? Are you sure?'

'Yes, because, as you gentlemen know, this was the king's games room.' He was directing his speech now at my companions and me, which I could see irritated Hosam. His mouth was open, hoping at any moment to resume his story. 'And the room is pretty much as it was then,' the waiter continued. 'The only additions are the bar and the piano. The chairs, gentleman, you are sitting in are also new, but they were modelled on pieces that were part of the palace furniture, however, not intended for this room, of course, for this, as I have already explained to Your Excellencies, was the snooker room, and therefore hardly had any furniture in it, or not nearly as many pieces as now.'

Hosam waved him away. The waiter bowed and said, 'But before I leave you, allow me to confirm that the armchairs, gentlemen, are of goat's leather, the highest quality.'

'Don't worry,' Hosam told him. 'We won't scratch them.'

'Your pardon, sir, it's not what I meant.'

'I know,' Hosam told him. 'Be at ease. What's your name?'

'Omar, Your Excellency.'

'Give this Excellency business a rest, Omar, and tell me, where are you from? And please don't say Zamalek. I detect an accent. Is it Al Munufia?'

'But, sir, you are so good?'

The obscurity of the waiter vanished. Now he was Omar from Al Munufia, a governorate in Lower Egypt. He bowed again and returned to the bar.

'The bastard,' Hosam said beneath his breath. 'Lecturing us.' Then, trying to read the time on his watch, he asked Mustafa, 'Aren't they supposed to be punctual, these Germans?' But then suddenly he looked beyond me and jumped to his feet.

When Mr Huffmyer reached our table Hosam gave a deep bow. The German looked bored. I excused myself, refusing Hosam's half-hearted invitation to remain, and sat with my book at a table on the opposite side of the bar.

Hosam's portrait of my father did not correspond to the man I knew. Nevertheless, I did not question its authenticity. I continued looking up at the chandelier, from a different angle now. I took note of the conversation Hosam was trying to have with the German. It was not difficult to hear because, as I later learnt, whenever Hosam spoke English his voice went up several decibels. I listened to him attempt to convince Mr Huffmyer of his 'experience' and 'astute abilities', and felt tenderness for Hosam when I heard him say that he would be 'a most honourable representative' for the Munich air-conditioning company. The silver head of the German remained still.

Although the lighting did not allow even the keenest of eyes to read, I opened my book. I had first read *Don Quixote* twelve years ago, when I was already a grown man. I came to it through a provocation I had read in one of the English literary journals. The reviewer – I have never been able to remember the Englishman's name – claimed that 'one ought only to read Miguel de Cervantes's *Don Quixote* as a child, well before the rivers of the mind have begun to set deeply into their banks. Reading it in maturity, when the currents of fantasy and reality are no longer able to mingle freely, would present a risk. What is lost in imaginative capacity in the reader would have to be compensated for with wilful, manual intent, which, given the wavering and equivocal methods that Cervantes employs, could unsettle the balance of a mature psyche. In fact,' the author went on, raising the stakes even higher, 'it is only when one has read the novel through the mental agility of early youth that one can hope to retain in manhood something of its childish wonder, for not having had the good fortune of reading it when young would invariably impoverish the imagination and leave it handicapped forever. Therefore, along with society's ordering classifications, such as that of gender, another significant demarcation needs to be made between those who have and those who have not read *Don Quixote* at youth.' And then, rubbing salt in the wound, the Englishman went on to tell us of his first reading, which took place when he was eight and when, according to his theory, the rivers of the mind are still shallow. His first encounter with the text was through Thomas Shelton's translation, the first translation of the text into any language, completed in 1612, when Cervantes was still alive. 'It was the rendition,' the reviewer went on, 'that Shakespeare would have read, if indeed he read *Don Quixote* at all. The record on this is inconclusive.'

Like my detractor, the author of that pessimistic article, I too am unable to read Spanish. But I have, in the past twelve years, tried to make up for both lost time and my lack of Spanish by reading every translation I could find in the two languages I possess, Arabic and English. The copy I keep in the glove compartment is Shelton's translation, partly because it was the first I had read and partly because I have never lost the thrill that Shakespeare's eyes might have followed the same words, in the same order.

The text did not enter the Arabic until more than a quarter-millennium after Cervantes's death, incomplete and through a suspicious route. It was published in Algeria in 1898. It was made from the French and not the Spanish. The copy I have omits the names of both the Arabic translator and the French one he followed. The language is archaic, which, I have not altogether stopped suspecting, might have been due to the fact that it was written not by an Arab, but by Cervantes himself, during his long years of imprisonment in Algeria, perhaps to help pass the time and amuse himself, and then left behind and discovered some nearly three centuries later, by an opportunist who did not speak Spanish but who, on account of the French occupation of Algeria, had French and therefore could claim the text as his own translation of a translation. A double mirror. Who knows? Well, I suppose the text knows. Which is why, regardless of its dubiousness, I have been returning from time to time to that partial Arabic translation of 1898, my interest sustained by the possibility that it was made by Cervantes.

I went to read by the light of the bar. The section I happened to open the book at was where Don Quixote, wearing his makeshift armour, approaches a castle and stops, expecting to hear the customary horn which heralds a knight's approach. At that exact moment, a swineherd blew his horn to gather the pigs and Don Quixote, 'with marvellous satisfaction of mind . . . approached to the inn and ladies.' Every time I read this it made me laugh, and this time was no different.

Hearing my own laughter, I blushed and decided to keep facing the page.

The German must have been speaking because Hosam and Mustafa were silent. I looked their way. They were as still as statues. Then Huffmyer stood up, tried to read his watch, and looked about with irritated impatience.

'But we have ordered all of this in your honour,' Hosam told him, pointing to the table. 'Then dinner tomorrow? But we insist . . . But this won't do. You will call me? Promise? Then I will forgive you, but only this once,' Hosam said and laughed too loudly. Hosam and Mustafa stood up and shook the man's hand. Hosam bowed deeply again. 'Goodbye, sir.' When the German was already walking away, Hosam called after him, 'And good night, Mr Huff . . . My regards to your excellent family.'

I faced the book again until Hosam touched my shoulder.

'Khaled Bey, honour us once again, please?' Then to the waiter, 'Omar, mint tea please.'

In the light I saw Hosam was not as old as I assumed. Disappointment wrinkled his brow, and that twitch was playing havoc now with his left eye in particular. I closed the book and he said, with sincere concern, 'Don't lose your place.' He had his hand tenderly cupping my elbow. 'Did you bend the corner of the page? Dog ears; isn't that what they call it in England? What a disappointment,' he said softly as we crossed the room.

'Welcome back, Khaled Bey,' Mustafa said. Then to Hosam: 'I told you; this Piano Bar place of yours is not the right location for a business meeting. He could hardly see the time. It's a bar for lovers.'

'And how am I supposed to know these things?' Hosam snapped.

'For a business meeting,' Mustafa said, directing his words towards me, 'you need a bright place where nothing is hidden. It gives people confidence.'

Hosam lit a cigarette. 'No, this has nothing to do with the venue; this has to do with cash. We obviously got to him too late. Someone had already whispered sweet promises in his ear. In Ali Pasha's days we never had to plead like this. Someone like this piece of German shit would have been begging for our services. We would go in, buy double the quantity of units anyone could purchase, sell them, then return with an even larger order, but with one condition: give us sole agency, not only in Egypt, but in the entire Middle East. This is how you do business. Otherwise, it is impossible to penetrate.'

'And what would you need to set up such a company?' I asked.

THE SECRET LIFE OF SHAKESPEAREANS

Soledad Puértolas
translated by Rosalind Harvey

I'm a man surrounded by Shakespeareans. My sister
Julia, who is a couple of years older than me, studied
English language and literature. She was in love with
the language of Shakespeare and, not surprisingly, she
then fell in love with Shakespeare, which, together with
her obvious natural attributes, prompted the group of
Shakespeareans – which wasn't small – to fall *en masse*
in love with her. As a result, a tightly bunched rosary of
boyfriends passed through her hands, and an endless
string of suitors filed through our house, some with
more flair than others.

I never got along with my sister's boyfriends, not so
much for being Shakespeareans, but because of their
qualities as boyfriends. The least clumsy of them was
far too shifty; the quiet one, whom you never knew how
to speak to, was as irritating as the chatterbox, whom
you could never get rid of.

Once she finished university, Julia didn't marry any of
them. Her eyes had fallen upon an economist, a young

man who read only in moderation. Essays, if anything. Never novels, let alone plays. But Shakespeare's presence in our family life did not cease, due not just to Julia's constant mentioning of him, marking out her conversation with lines from his plays – particularly his lesser-known ones, just to intimidate us – but also to the simple tendency my sister had to turn her life into a stage play. She had of course been born with this trait, but no one doubted that Shakespeare had contributed enormously to its development.

Julia and Marco got married, had two children, and seem like a well-matched couple. We all get on well with Marco. He's a consultant for a large firm and his task, as far as I can tell, consists of improving product sales. Something to do with efficiency and the company's image, I think. Anyway, the thing is, he travels a lot, he's been to almost every country in the world.

When we talk to Marco about news from wars that seem a long way off, he gives us new facts. He knows this city, that region, he tells us something about them, the food, the smells, anything. Not just wars and catastrophes: his comments might also allude to happy events. But we all know what the news is like – it doesn't relay a huge amount of happiness.

Sometimes, Julia and I both show up at our parents' house for dinner. The time when it was just the two of us with them around the dining-room table, and our bedrooms, mine and Julia's, were each on one side of the hall, is long gone, but we are the same: the same parents, the same son and daughter. Just like always, but after a period of time. The two of us speaking much more than they do, now. The two of them looking at us much more than they ever have done. With curiosity, with an awareness of a certain distance, conscious they will never fully know us. Accepting it, perhaps eagerly, as if shrugging off a weight.

One of these nights, after eating, we settled down in the living room to slowly drink our coffee. Our parents had both put their heads back and closed their eyes. They dozed. On the TV, we'd just watched images of houses destroyed by bombs, columns of smoke, men crawling through the dust, among the wreckage, gunshots.

'Aleppo,' Julia murmured. 'We were there five years ago. That was when I used to go with Marco on quite a few of his trips. I used to enjoy it. The firms Marco did business with sorted everything out for us. They put us up in five-star hotels and there was always a car with a driver for me to use, and a guide to show me around the monuments and other interesting places in the cities. I had lots of spare time but I never got bored. I liked the hotel restaurants. I liked watching the other travellers. A strange thing happened to me in Aleppo.'

I made a mental note of everything Julia told me. Like the excellent amateur actress she is, she has a real knack for telling stories. She knows I like listening to her and that I often use the anecdotes she tells me in my novels, transformed, put into someone else's mouth. Before she begins, she usually says to me: 'This might interest you, you'll figure out the best way to use it.'

Later that evening, I wrote down what Julia had told me (and dramatised, too) at our parents' house. I hardly changed a thing. I liked it just as it had happened. This is her story.

The driver left me in front of one of the gates to the bazaar in Aleppo and, while I waited for him (I don't know if he had gone to park the four-by-four somewhere else or whether he had to do something, get money from the bank or an ATM or buy tobacco, I can't remember), I went into a shop whose little window display was full of fine scarves in all the colours of the rainbow. Up above, and to both sides of the door, hung more scarves like the others. Scarves of every size, made from silk, from very fine wool, from cotton. The breeze filled them up and blew them to and fro. It was impossible to resist the temptation to go into the shop. I rang the driver – he was guide and driver in one – and he agreed to come and meet me in the shop right away.

I lost myself among all those scarves. When the guide turned up, the owner of the shop, a charming man with a white beard, a djellaba and a crimson-coloured fez, was still making up the parcels.

Since we planned to take a good long look around the bazaar, the guide asked the shopkeeper to look after the bag with the scarves for me so I could walk round with my hands free, essential in a bazaar where there's so much to see, to poke about in, to touch. He agreed happily, as far as we could tell from the great big smile he gave us. He stood in the doorway to the shop, looking around with satisfaction.

When I emerged from the bazaar, one or two hours later – an indeterminate amount of time, as labyrinthine and repetitive as the hours spent on a stage – I felt so exhausted I almost forgot about the scarves being held for me in the shop. My guide didn't, though. To him, my confusion made sense.

'It's true, bazaars make you dizzy,' he said. 'Your thoughts go all over the place, some go and others come in their place. It's a healthy movement,' he said. 'It's life.'

I felt something very special, as if I were in a play, something I had sensed a few hours earlier, in the same shop at the entrance to the bazaar, as I got lost among the colours, sizes and textures of the scarves. Absorbed in a reality that made me desire everything and doubt everything at once, and which emptied me out of my previous life, of the connections in it, of the trip itself and my role in it. I existed there like I had never existed anywhere else. I was touching something unique, transcendent. Something that went beyond life.

And so we went back to the shop with the scarves. The man with the crimson fez and the leathery skin handed us the bag and said goodbye again from the entrance to the shop, leaning against the doorway, encircled by a crown of scarves swollen in the wind like sails, happy and full.

Back at the hotel, I left the packages in my room, freshened up a little and went down to eat in the restaurant. Then I fell asleep. Later that evening, I took the packages out of the bag and opened them. In one of the bundles, instead of one silk scarf, there were two. Exactly the same. Clinging to each other. Duplicated. A mistake. Or was it?

That night, over dinner, I mentioned it to Marco. How could it be that an old Syrian shopkeeper whose premises backed on to one of the most ancient bazaars in the world had made a mistake?

'It's because he wants you to go back. It's a sort of test,' Marco said, jokingly, knowing full well that this was exactly what I wanted to hear.

I decided that it wasn't my place to teach anyone a lesson, still less an old shopkeeper from Aleppo. I would go back to the shop, buy another silk scarf, show him I knew when to keep my mouth shut, that I'd come back to set something right, if he wanted to do so, that is.

I gave no explanation to the guide. All I said was that I wanted to return to the shop, which didn't surprise him. He smiled, and nodded his head, as if saying to himself, 'Yes, I knew it, I knew we'd go back.'

Once again I was in the shop. A sunny morning. The wind was blowing; the scarves fluttered.

The old man wasn't surprised to see me. Once again he showed me some scarves, opening drawers, sliding display trays out, unfolding pieces of cloth.

'This is the finest shawl of them all,' he said, placing his wrinkled, bony hand on a piece of cashmere fabric in pinkish hues.

Then, he moved his hand to his neck, just below his chin.

'This is where the wool is at its finest. There's nothing softer.'

I asked him the price, which seemed to me exorbitant.

'You won't find a shawl like this anywhere else,' he said, or at least I thought I understood.

I bought it – how could I not? Why had I gone back to the shop, otherwise?

It was the last purchase I made on that trip.

Nevertheless, this incomparable shawl got ruined. Some-one (maybe one of the maids who came to clean the house and who generally, more than any other job, used to like doing the laundry) put it in the washing machine. The shawl shrunk, the fabric grew tight and became matted, the edges curled slightly, the pink tones lost something of their delicate contrast.

The best shawl that the old shopkeeper from Aleppo could offer me, bought on my second visit to his shop, after having found among my purchases one handkerchief too many.

A question arose, of course: was the shawl that excep-tional? It shouldn't have been put in the washing machine, naturally, but was it really extraordinary, unique? Was it worth the high price I had paid for it?

It was a real anecdote, and I tried to respect it just as it was. I carried it inside me; I'd find out soon enough what I might do with it. It was too closely linked to my sister to attribute it, unaltered, to another character.

One day, I run into Ignacio Gil, one of those Shakespearean boyfriends of Julia's who had trooped unsuccessfully through our house. Of them all, he had perhaps been the best. Very modest, profoundly shy, somewhat evasive. He had become a renowned specialist on Shakespeare.

We have a coffee in a nearby bar and, without letting me get a word in edgeways (not that I would have known what to say), he launches into a long and tedious speech on the question of Shakespeare's identity. He does not put the man's identity into question, what interests him is why so many doubts have arisen, why people have tried so hard to prove that Shakespeare wasn't Shakespeare but someone else, a Bacon, an Earl of Oxford, a Lady So-and-So.

Later on, after countless theories about one or another aspect of Shakespeare's oeuvre, he asks me about my sister. Wanting to make the most of it being my turn, and because I enjoyed the anecdote and felt like telling it, I slowly string out the story of Julia and the scarves of Aleppo, the cashmere shawl, the shopkeeper with his crimson-coloured fez.

Ignacio Gil listens very closely, fervently, I would say, as if he doesn't want to miss a single detail, which makes me drag my tale out, making it longer, although I do try to stick to the story. When I finish, Ignacio Gil looks at me with a strange expression, as if he'd had a vision, a vision of the very same bazaar in Aleppo or the shop with the silk scarves. Then he asks me for my phone number, which he stores in his mobile phone. He gives me his and watches, silently, as I type it in.

It's very hot out in the street and we move away from each other with scarcely another word. I can't stop wondering why he suddenly went so quiet, why he made not a single comment about Julia's anecdote.

Two days later, he calls me. In truth, I'm not surprised.

We've arranged to meet on the terrace outside a bar. It's nine o'clock at night. The heat persists, but there is a gentle breeze, not exactly cool, but not boiling hot, either.

I arrive punctually. I don't mind waiting. This is when my mind is at its busiest. I take my Moleskine from my pocket and assume the exact appearance of a writer with no time to waste. I see Ignacio Gil approaching between the tables. He's very pale. We all are, those of us who don't have swimming pools, who spend this first month of the summer partly shut up in our houses and offices. But Ignacio Gil's paleness is something else. He has a panicked expression on his face.

'It's a disaster!' he says, almost before sitting down, without even saying hello. 'Look at my hair.'

I look at his head, the dark brown hair. Artificial, obviously dyed.

'I just don't know how I let myself be talked into it,' he says. 'It was my daughter Ana's idea. It was a stupid thing to do. A man like me with his hair dyed . . . how could I let something like this happen? But Ana insisted. According to her, the colour will fade with time, the more I wash it, and it'll end up perfect, although I don't know when. I've washed my hair about ten times and it's still black, as you can see. It's totally ridiculous, it's inappropriate. I'm so embarrassed.'

'Plenty of men dye their hair,' I tell him. 'No one's shocked by that nowadays. And anyway, the colour will fade, sooner or later. It's a matter of time.'

'I have to accept it, I know – I've got old,' Ignacio says. 'I suppose that's what the problem is.'

The waiter comes over. Ignacio Gil orders a beer. He sighs. In the slightly hushed tone used for secrets, he says:

'What you told me the other day about your sister, that thing that happened to her in that city, Aleppo, I've been thinking about it – do you believe in symbols? I don't know, it seemed like a really symbolic story to me. What do they represent, the two silk scarves? And the ruined shawl that cost an exorbitant amount? And the old man with the maroon fez? What role does he play in the story? Was he the one who pulled the strings or was it controlled from higher up, from who knows where?'

'It's something that happened,' I say, 'something real. It sounds poetic, magical, even, when it's told as a story.'

'Maybe,' he said, not very convinced. 'Does Julia tell you lots of things? That's a stroke of luck, isn't it? Being a writer and having people tell you things you then go on to tell. What about Julia? How is she? The two of you are pretty close, aren't you? Anyway, I don't know, the story about the silk scarves really affected me. Time suddenly closed in on me, I don't know why. I felt very old, like I was already on life's edge. It was like a pang of nostalgia, who knows, nostalgia for my lost youth. You can't go back, you just can't. Your sister feeling doubtful as she looked at those two scarves, I liked that, I really did. I'm like that too, I never know what to do. I don't know what I would have done in her place; maybe I would have gone back too, like she did, gone back to the shop and bought something else, just to pretend nothing had happened, so as not to feel guilty. I understand her, I do, I understand why she did what she did. That's what moved me, as if that ability, to understand someone, was something that suddenly revealed itself to me, something being resurrected. It had left me and it came back. That's why I was moved, but moved with a really sad emotion, a kind of anguish. That was when Ana appeared, and started talking to me about dying my hair. She'd been telling me to do it for ages. "You can't put it off any longer, Dad," she said. I couldn't say no. I had to do something, I felt awful.'

'You can't really tell,' I said, lying. 'You just look a bit paler. When I saw you, I thought something had happened to you. It's done now, don't take it so seriously.'

'I can't fix it, I'm too ashamed,' he says. 'As soon as I see someone I tell them, I want to get in there before they say anything, I want them to know I'm aware of the mistake, that I'm embarrassed.'

'You could always shave your head,' I say, thinking that this, in his place, is what I would do, although I can't imagine myself in his place at all.

The fact is that Ignacio Gil's remorse touched me. I could see him walking down the corridors of the Faculty of Philosophy, where he teaches, giving explanations for his hair left, right and centre. He would rather get in there first, make a statement, than have to make an embarrassing confession; like the child who, after committing some small crime, fears being discovered and announces his innocence prematurely, suspiciously. I understood him, just as he understood Julia when, after seeing the two silk scarves in her hotel room, she went back to the shop.

Beneath all this is what matters. It was the anecdote about the scarves in Aleppo that led Ignacio Gil to dye his hair.

'There's nothing interesting in my life,' he says, in a tiny little voice. 'I have a friend, Gerardo, who's had lots of adventures, some very odd things have happened to him, incredible things. The next time you and I meet up, if you've got time, I'll tell you some of these stories, you could write a novel with them, several novels even.'

'I'm not an epic writer, Ignacio,' I say. 'I'm more interested in the subject of your hair.'

He looked at me, his eyes very wide in the middle of his white face, probably convinced I was teasing him.

I told my sister about my encounters with her old Shakespearean boyfriend. One of them. The best, without a doubt.

'Why do you think he rang me?' I asked her.

'He probably wants to be your friend. Maybe he feels lonely.'

'It's because of you,' I said. 'All that stuff about dying his hair after I talked to him about you, well – it's pretty obvious, his memory of you stirred something up, he wanted to be young again. You'd better watch out, any day now you'll run into him and he'll try and ask you out again.'

'He always was quite an elusive guy,' Julia said. 'But not totally elusive, not totally . . . I might have been more elusive than he was. I never thought he'd end up becoming a scholar. He's an authority on Shakespeare. I didn't see that coming.'

The thing is, Ignacio Gil doesn't call me again. It's not that I miss him, but in a way, his story, the one about the dyed hair, had interested me and probably his relationship with my sister had, too.

In the middle of summer, sitting out on the terrace of a bar, my Moleskine on the table and my head empty, or too full, but of heavy, useless things, I slide my finger over the screen of my mobile phone. Ignacio Gil.

'How's the hair?' I ask.

'Oh, the hair, yeah, much better! I'll call you back, I'm driving.'

He hangs up and calls me back a minute later.

'Where are you?' he asks. 'I'll be with you in ten minutes.'

It's curious, but as I wait for Ignacio Gil – slightly longer than ten minutes – I have the impression I'm waiting for a great friend, someone I really trust.

He's not so pale any more. His hair isn't completely black, it has a more muted tone, more matt. Ignacio Gil is looking good. He looks younger. If I told him this, he'd be pleased, but I don't. I don't really know why, but I keep quiet. In any case, he already seems pretty pleased.

'You haven't left either,' he says. 'This city is great in the summer. I'm so happy I stayed. Laura and the kids are at the beach, but I have to finish off a translation.'

'Shakespeare?'

'Of course. It's never-ending, you can always improve it.'

'Have you been thinking about the Aleppo scarves, about everything that happened to Julia and that you thought was so symbolic?'

He smiles with forced indifference, and shakes his head.

'Occupational hazard,' he says. 'We students of literature are always looking for symbols in everything.'

'The most interesting thing about that anecdote,' I say, 'is Julia herself. Her doubts, her suspicions, the decisions she makes, perhaps the wrong ones.'

He looks vague. He might agree with me, he might not. It doesn't matter. It's ancient history now. He's tied up in other matters. Shakespeare again, those kings out of context, those improbable scenarios, those exaggerated passions, those manipulators, so evil, or the professional scroungers, the cynics, the egotists, that capacity of Shakespeare's to go from one to the other, casting a net of captivating lines that is hoisted higher and higher. Ignacio Gil is, without a doubt, at his peak as an orator, as an academic lecturer. Occasionally, there is a phrase in English that he intones slowly, accompanied by gestures. He raises his arms up a little, separating his hands, and traces a circle in the air, a magnificent sphere that encompasses everything.

He has cast a net out towards me, his own net of words, interlaced on top of Shakespeare's words, but I am an experienced observer. Ignacio Gil is euphoric, that's what matters.

I say goodbye, but he stays where he is. He's not in a hurry, he says. He's on his own in Madrid. He'll have a drink somewhere and then go home and work some more. A long night of intense work awaits him.

I could have told him that I'm on my own in Madrid too, suggest we have a drink together, but I know that Ignacio Gil would carry on talking about Shakespeare, would hardly let me speak, that the night would be for him, for his monologue.

It's then that I realise Ignacio Gil hasn't asked me about Julia.

Maybe I'll leave Madrid. I'm tired of this heat. The advantages of the empty city aren't enough for me – not exactly empty, just with fewer people and less traffic – but I don't know what I could do, with whom or where to go. I make a few phone calls. When I go to sleep – or try to – at around two in the morning, the blanket of heat seems to have dissolved and an almost-magical, soft breeze is blowing, incredibly fragile and destined, without a doubt, for a very fleeting life. I now have some kind of prospect, a journey to the north in the company of another solitary traveller.

My parents are still in Madrid. A few years ago they installed air conditioning in their seventh-floor apartment, at the very top of the building. They don't mind, they say, staying in the city for all of August. You can't go anywhere in August. The hotels are full, the beaches overflowing. They wait until September. They spend a fortnight in a hotel. They always choose the south, Almería or Cádiz. Portugal, occasionally. They go with another married couple, my mother's younger brother and his wife. They have a lovely time. They argue a little about the quality of the wine they order with their meals. My mother's younger brother and his wife have become very demanding and order expensive wines, which upsets my parents' budget. They try to negotiate, to reach an agreement. OK, we'll spend a little more on the wine for you guys. In return, let's visit some churches today. My father's passion: little shrines in secluded mountain gullies, ancient, enigmatic constructions of brick, who knows what they hold or what was made there, ruins in the middle of the countryside. Visiting churches includes all this.

I call my mother and tell her to expect me at dinner.

'I think I'll leave tomorrow,' I say. 'I'll come and say goodbye first.'

I spend the morning writing. That is, having breakfast, reading the paper, showering, drinking coffee, walking around the house, sitting in front of my computer, getting up, checking my emails, checking something on the internet.

I decide to walk to my parents' house. I take the shady side of the street. The breeze from last night, the fleeting one, is still fluttering, its life happily prolonged. I feel like leaving, losing sight of this city for a few days, leaving aside my grand literary projects, my wandering around the house waiting for important calls, proposals, plaudits, prizes (oh God, sometimes I dream of prizes, too!). Swimming in the sea, in the freezing water of the north, where my friend has a house, gazing at the trees, the orchards, the vineyards, the parks, the gardens.

My mother opens the door. She looks very pleased to see me, as if rather than the five or six days that have passed since we saw each other, a whole year had gone by.

'Where are you off to, then?' she asks.

'Galicia,' I say. 'I'm going with Adrian, to the house he has there. He couldn't really be bothered to go, but it's different when someone goes with you, we both warmed to the idea.'

The phone rings.

'How nice, darling! What a lovely surprise!' I hear my mother say. 'Of course we'll wait for you. Your brother's here too, he's just arrived, he's off tomorrow. This is such a coincidence, now you two can see each other.'

My mother, evidently, is speaking to Julia. She puts down the phone and looks at us.

'Julia is in Madrid. She got here this morning. She had to do something at the boys' school, something about the curriculum there, I didn't fully understand; anyway, the thing is she's on her way, she'll be here any minute. Now you two can see each other,' she says again, the same phrase she ended her phone call with.

Julia has come to Madrid for a few hours and I'm still in Madrid, this is the only thing that matters to my mother. The rest is unimportant. My mother's great joy comes from Julia and I seeing each other, sitting together around the dining room table under her satisfied gaze, as if the two of us being there, by her side, were a guarantee of something, of some sort of continuity, beyond plans and personal wishes, something transcendent that will last forever.

'Now you two can see each other,' she repeats. A simple phrase, a kind of mantra.

I had my own mantra, made up of images: Ignacio Gil listening in fervent silence and with pensive, melancholy gaze to the story of the scarves of Aleppo; his pale face a few days later, in unnerving contrast to his dyed black hair, his shame and the nostalgia for his youth; the euphoria of yesterday, as he spoke about Shakespeare, not an atom of nostalgia by then, alone in the city abandoned for the summer, far from his wife and from his children. This, as a logical continuation of the story, was where Julia's unexpected arrival slotted in.

Unexpected and fleeting. Julia turned up late, just as we were about to sit down at the table, and left immediately, not staying for coffee. She said she had lots of things to do. Errands, things that Marco and the kids had asked her to do, she had very little time. I felt like she was lying, that the voice she said all this in was not her own. Her voice, her eyes, her gestures, her smile, everything was different.

EGYPTIAN PUPPET

Vicente Molina Foix
translated by Frank Wynne

She had enjoyed it more than he had, though the man had wept at the end. They made their way down from the balcony with the rest of the crowd, she walking slightly ahead of him; outside the rain was waiting, a heavy curtain curious as to who would part it and who would baulk. Some braved the torrent, sheltering themselves as best they could, but the couple paused for a moment beneath the stone archway. 'By providence the heavens kept the rains away until the play was done.' The man smiled and shook his head. 'It rained half an hour ago. When the Roman climbed the tree to watch the battle. A drop or two, no more. I saw them splash upon the railing.' 'Perhaps it was but your tears you saw?'

The rain was lashing harder as they crossed the bridge and arrived home, their faces and arms wet, their clothes sodden. It was the second day of August, and though their summer clothes afforded little protection, they were easily removed. Both were naked now, the man kneeling before the hearth to light the fire. The woman hugged him from behind, her fingers running over his lips, covering his eyes, tousling his hair as she stared into the first flames that licked the logs, which were slow to catch as though the damp had seeped from the man's skin. His felt hat lay at his feet, crushed by the weight of the rain that had fallen on it.

'Why did you weep?'

'For her. Others wept. You shed no tears, being a woman.'

'I never weep, however fine the players.'

'I do not understand why she acted so.'

'In taking her life?'

'In suffering. She was beloved by the most eminent men of the age. And the Roman suffered too.'

'He had to suffer; he betrayed her.'

'And I cannot understand why ancient tales of love must end in death. Do you remember the youthful lovers of Verona in the sepulchre? No one now dies such a death.'

It took them some little time to fall asleep, her more so than him, he drifted off as soon as the firewood ceased its crackling. When first his eyes closed, the woman thought he was pretending and stealthily drew nearer, fluttering her hand between his brow and his lips; he began to breathe quietly. She turned away from him in the bed and lay, still wakeful, until his childlike breath lulled her to sleep.

She was roused by the sun stealing past the shutters they had forgotten to close the night before in their haste to dry themselves and restage the amorous frolics of the Queen and the Triumvir on their narrow mattress, that dance of beaded skirt and heavy doublet in a painted palace. Today was Sunday, and they had no cause to venture abroad, yet his eyes opened when he felt the same ray of sunlight and heard the bells of St Mary-le-Bow toll seven of the clock, then, without returning her kiss, he leapt from the bed, pulled on shirt and breeches and stumbled across the yard to the privy; no sooner had he returned than he was eager to be gone, with not a morsel to eat, with not a kiss for her. What could he be doing on the Sabbath, when he was not called to work at the gaol?

'A gaol does not close, and there are some fellows would toast my birthday. Will you call upon your sister? I shall be home late.'

Night drew in and still the man had not returned; lying awake in bed, Margaret waited. When she heard the first footfalls in the street below, and the voice of a woman chiding a querulous child, she rose and went to her embroidery frame; she had four kerchiefs to furnish for a marriage on Thursday but did not feel disposed to work. When eight bells rang at St Mary-le-Bow, she left the house and walked to Newgate Prison where she sought out Cyril, who, like her husband, had been raised in the West Riding and was the only gaoler she knew by name. Today, they were to execute a priest found guilty of treason and conspiracy against the Crown and a great crowd had massed before the gates. Whole families had come up from the country, the men still garbed in muddy work clothes; noblemen with ready sneezes had reserved seats in the stands, while dogs prowled in search of a master or some gobbet of meat. A cohort of magistrates, stripped of their robes, stood apart from the throng to make it known that they would watch this grisly spectacle only in the service of the law. Margaret became lost among the teeming crowd of women come in search of wayward drunken husbands who had not been seen these two nights since, not even floating in the river, or lawless sons wounded in some tavern brawl on Saturday whom they yet hoped might languish in the cells and not the morgue.

Just then, she spied Cyril at one of the prison gates and strode to meet him; he knew her face and played the gallant for much that she was dishevelled. Thomas had not been seen on Sunday, he said, nor had he appeared this morning at his post, indeed the head watchman was much vexed and had enquired as to his whereabouts. 'And it is queer he should not come this morning,' Cyril's voice dropped to a whisper, 'when such a notable execution is to be held. We gaolers earn more on certain special days. The common folk and even those sorry wretches behind bars are all dying for a glimpse of the condemned man, and will gladly pay to watch the spectacle. If you wish, you shall have a front row seat over in that corner. From there, you shall see the traitor's purple tongue loll out as though he died for you alone.'

She made no answer but left the prison, discomfited, taking swift strides as though the legs concealed beneath her voluminous skirts were the only living part of her, the only part able to challenge, to take decisions.

What yet remains within me? You alone remain.

She passed St Stephen's Church, where as a child she had prayed in terrified silence as she gazed upon the image of the martyr stoned by brutes, their doublets all unbraced; these days, she no longer feared the stones, nor the powerful muscles of the executioners, but St Stephen, as he knelt and prayed, was now but a distant consolation of the hereafter.

Close to hand lived Jane, her older sister, who per-formed miracles within and without the bodies of women. To those desirous of capturing the attentions of some gentleman, Jane could furnish treacle poultices to firm the breasts, almond milk simmered with spices from India and pastilles of candied flowers to counter the foul breath of age and rotting teeth; the receipts of Mr Morgan, the apothecary who had long served the late queen, were still in great demand at the Cheapside dispensary, though it was Jane who now prepared them in the back room of the shop. From time to time, a flustered manservant would appear at the counter, stammering that his mistress was in need of the 'other Jane', the accommodating midwife, the gatherer of simples, she whose occult remedies were fashioned not to beautify but to destroy something that was growing in the lady yet had no rightful name. Margaret had no need of such physic. She walked on through Walbrook, further and further from her empty home and from Jane and her skilled hands. She came to the banks of the river. On the far shore was the circular theatre, the stone archway where they had sheltered from the rain, the words they each had spoken, the verses they had listened to together.

In the afternoon, in the sun's declining hour, she sat once again at her embroidery frame and there she worked to finish the wedding kerchiefs some prosperous landowners from Twickenham were to give as keepsakes to the most illustrious guests at their wedding. She made the final stitches: crimson silk thread for the berries and, at the base of the burgeoning plant, a tangle of rough, twisted roots, an addition over which she took great pains.

On Thursday, having delivered the embroidered kerchiefs to her patron Mr Gibbons, she made the self-same journey she had made three days before, cast a hateful glance upon the swiftly flowing waters as they swept flinders and flotsam in their wake, but not one corpse, then she headed south across the bridge to the theatre. On Tuesday night, she had seen Thomas appear atop the turret of the theatre in a dream, signalling with a pennant, another woman standing next to him. Now, at the top of the Globe Playhouse, there was only a bare flagstaff: no pennant, no woman, no Thomas. On the esplanade by the stone archway some boys were playing with a ball of rags and string. It was an idle entertainment requiring little effort, with no rivalry, no victors, one that seemed to have no greater goal than to keep the ball sailing into the air, where it tarried a moment before it fell, never to the ground, never swiftly. One of the lads would leap up, catch it, and with a blow from his open palm thrust it towards the heavens. Seeing this beautiful stranger walking in circles and watching them, these angels hurled curses and imprecations, hands cupping the bulges in their breeches that marked them out as men.

On that Thursday, The King's Men were performing a comedy shown the previous winter at the Globe Playhouse, *Volpone; or, the Fox*. The play, according to a widow with dyed hair come from Oxford to see it for the second time, was comical, merely comical, with ne'er a hint of tragedy nor a drop of spilt blood. 'In the play this afternoon, there are none but scoundrels and mountebanks, but tomorrow they play another that I shall also come to see, a courtly tale of wooing in a French forest where all are dressed as others than themselves. This is what I prize above all. This roguish world of the living that I intend to be part of as long as my legs will bear me and there is laughter in my body. Buy a covered seat before there are no more. You shall see we will come out fresh-faced with nary a tear.' Margaret thanked the woman and went on her way.

How can I go in alone? I have never gone to the theatre alone. Only with you. You were my favourite companion, though you did not know how to dissemble. I do not know either.

Life for Margaret dragged out long and bitter. She left the little house on Ironmongers Lane, it being too large for her needs, and moved into a cramped room two doors from the apothecary where her sister brewed potions and slept upstairs. They spent their evenings together, living like spinsters though both had husbands. Jane's was in the Navy Royal but, being his sister-in-law, Margaret had seen him only twice, at weddings; her sister's to the seaman and her own to the gaoler, whom the naval officer had eyed scornfully: a clash of uniforms. 'I never know where the rascal is,' Jane mused one night when her heart weighed sadly. 'Where might he be today? Off the coast of Barbary, perhaps, or sailing closer by to spy on Spaniards.'

Where are you, Thomas Vaughan, now you are not watching o'er your prisoners? Each morning I go to know whether you have returned, well inclined to credit any excuse you choose to give me, but you are never there. The mothers and the daughters of the prisoners now greet me piteously, surmising from my grief that my husband must be a murderer of children or some rabble-rousing papist.

The Welshman who had taken Thomas's post made

clear to Margaret that he was indifferent to her absent husband. He was enthralled by her serenity of gait and speech, her slender hands, to say nothing of what he supposed beneath her skirts. They could live together, and by their thrift spare the cost of two households. Yes or no?

'No,' was her sole response. She was not free, nor did she desire the presence of another man.

Someone has left, but he has not left me. Thomas will return.

She accepted another job of work from Mr Gibbons, knowing it to be the last. It was an heraldic panel on which she was to broider the arms and likeness of the duke who had commanded it. For many hours and days Margaret laboured upon the design that lay next to her embroidery frame: the sea swell, the furling waves that symbolised the nobleman's distant voyages, the wild animal and the great fishes he had killed and brought back, anatomised, to England, and in one corner a portrait of his mother embodied as the goddess Juno. But in the central portrait of the duke, Margaret took certain liberties. She fashioned a fantastical body, half man, half beast, which being heroic and as virile struck Mr Gibbons as somewhat bombastic, though exquisitely stitched. 'Fine work. Ill-judged.' He paid her for the piece, but dismissed her. And thus she found herself more free and in greater need.

Her sister proposed that she work at the apothecary, offered to teach her how to prepare beautifying unctions, long-lasting perfumes, stimulating tonics, tinctures to relieve pain, and narcotics – the span and compass of the herbalist's pharmacopoeia. As to expelling the sinful fruits of the womb, Jane alone would tend to such matters. Margaret consented to work there for one week when her sister's sailor husband arrived home unannounced, his ship having lately docked in Portsmouth, eager to celebrate with his wife his recent preferment to the rank of boatswain. They travelled to the Lakes and, upon their return, the husband bade farewell and rejoined his galleon; Jane, for her part, seemed another woman, one of those same gentlewomen she ministered to with her sure hands. In that week, Margaret had versed herself in the many essences and had devised a receipt for a syrup of liquorice that provoked immediate laughter and, its effect passed, did not lead to prostration. Thus, finding herself contented, she resolved to remain in service at Mr Morgan's apothecary shop, which welcomed her gladly.

One morning, towards midday, a carriage drawn by two horses in fine livery stopped outside the dispensary and there entered three men and a youth, the latter mewling and kicking. The boy did not wish to have his face powdered nor his cheeks painted with ladies' cosmetics, but his father, the eldest of the men, commanded. He had paternal authority, the other two had money, and the younger of these, from what Margaret could surmise, was chief among The King's Men who

were presently to stage a new work. On seeing Margaret with the pomade in hand, the boy became calm as
though a woman whitening the shadow of his downy
beard was no threat to his manhood. He was a handsome lad, though graceless and surly of manner, but
a lotion of milk and butter and a curling of his lashes
gave him a gentleness that tempered his gaucheness.
That very afternoon, he was to play the princess in a
tragedy wherein a whole family would perish by reason
of a foolish inheritance. In gratitude to Margaret for
her patience with the boy, the leader of the company
invited her to see the afternoon's performance. 'So you
may weep free of cost.' She demurred. She did not care
for theatre. Nor for weeping.

She became a young woman who, according to the
hours, hated and loved a man. At nightfall, her sister
could make her forget her sorrows with waggish tales
of what had happened in the day, since often the most
notorious ladies among her customers received her in
their chambers so that, in secret, she might display
the full range of her beautifying potions; one duchess,
frustrated by her duke's faltering desire, and having
heard tell from an Italian in Cambridge of a rare device,
asked whether Jane could procure a simulacrum of
the female genitals fashioned from wax and honey,
which, when placed atop the real thing gripped the
male member so firmly that its owner never wished to
withdraw and would sometimes fall to sleep *homo erectus.*

Jane had never heard of such a thing, but invented a less extravagant version of the same, just as, to regale her sister, she invented incidents where soldiers returning from battle came to her so she might heal their privates, they having exposed the same – believing it to cure purulent infection – to the scorching sun of Portugal, which left many impotent, and the more pertinacious incontinent. On nights of such drollery, she would sleep often five or six hours at a stretch, only to wake before the day, missing the childlike breath of her husband; not hearing him next to her kindled such heartbreak as might be assuaged by tears dabbed with a handkerchief. Alas she could not weep. Not even at the tragedies of others.

Time did pass, and one afternoon when her sister's work called her from London, she went again to the theatre. To brood in the theatre. She remembered that soon after their wedding day, Thomas had taken her across the river to see a comedy set in the impossible kingdom of Navarre, and when in the five years of their marriage they had returned to the Globe Playhouse once or twice each summer, how she had delighted to see those plays that unfolded on imagined isles or in lands so ancient they might well be counterfeit. In suffering or in joy, the strangeness of the characters, their fantastical attire, the conjured names of cities yet unheard all seemed to her the stuff of magic, of winter's tales. So it was that she had allowed him to take her to the grand tragedy that they had seen on the day that Thomas marked thirty years, the day before he left their home never to return. She so despised that day she had forgot the name and the argument of that historic tale set in some far-off land. She remembered two words only: Egyptian puppet.

Where is Egypt?

The sun had emerged after five long weeks slumbering among the clouds that lour until springtime, and the crowds were beginning to gather on the esplanade before the playhouse where, when Margaret first arrived, there were but three beggars and a woman bringing the players' garments. People came from north and south, by foot and in coaches that waited in the alleys for their masters or left once unburdened of their travellers. Riotous they were, all clamouring together. 'A joyous rabble,' she thought. 'Today they play a tragedy of love,' she heard a woman's voice whisper in her ear. 'A love that truly happened beneath an Orient moon that first blessed then doomed the lovers.'

Turning, she recognised beneath the high falsetto the peevish boy that she had painted, that pale skin she had flushed with red, those eyes that with her own hands she had made a wide and dazzling black with pencil. 'Are you alone?' 'I am never alone. My ladies are with me. At first I did not like it, I played small roles, peasant women or nurses in rude garb. The day you painted me, I played my first young lady; the daughter of a foolish king who bequeaths his lands to her spiteful sisters. Since that day, I have been Juliet and Cressida, the ill-starred Venetian lass strangled by the Moor and bold Rosalind who feigns she is a man. And today . . . ' 'Today?' 'Today I return since, for the first time in two years, they will play the tragedy of Antony and Cleopatra. Have you no husband to escort you? My name is Nicholas. Nicko, they call me.'

Margaret watched the performance alone, standing near the front of the unroofed yard, as though the story of these wayward lovers, these jealousies, these tricks, these wars fought in bedchamber and on battlefield were new to her. The actor playing Mark Antony was a handsome man who, as he whispered passionately to Cleopatra, gazed at the women in the crowd as though he would seduce them. This did not trouble her, nor did his Scottish accent. Margaret had eyes only for Nicko.

By now, Antony was dead, and Margaret felt it was just that he die by his own hand, by his own sword as the actor reeled and staggered so much among the candles he seemed about to set his tunic ablaze. The climax of the tragedy was yet to come. The grief of Cleopatra. The vanities of sovereigns. The boy actor spoke the words in a still, soft voice, arms by his sides, no waving or gesticulation, no queenly raiment but a plain white tunic like that worn by her maidservant Iras, to whom Nicko announced the humiliation the victors were preparing to visit on her and on her mistress.

> Thou, an Egyptian puppet, shalt be shown
> In Rome, as well as I. Mechanic slaves
> With greasy aprons, rules, and hammers, shall
> Uplift us to the view.

This was the same Cleopatra who stood upon the stage, her bare feet those of a boy, showing herself to the people of Rome, to the scholars standing behind Margaret who had laughed at the words 'Egyptian puppet', to the rude peasant who fell upon the floor in fear when he saw Nicko pluck a writhing serpent from a basket of figs. Standing downstage, the queen allowed her maidservants to bedeck her with jewels, her robe of state, her crown; she seemed to hear Antony call to her. Husband, I come.

She saw how Cleopatra wept for love, and how she died for love, as Nicko pressed the sharp teeth of the viper to his false breast.

> The stroke of death is as a lover's pinch,
> Which hurts, and is desired.

Margaret was the last of the much-moved spectators to leave, and she tarried in the playhouse by a stair. There was no one to be seen now. And so she dared ascend the steps, and draw back a curtain which gave onto a chamber with a door; this she opened, to the surprise of three naked boys, the three maidservants in the tragedy, tossing the basket of figs between them as though it were a ball. Nicko was not among them. She asked after him, but the jeering lads said they knew no one by that name. Perchance she sought Cleopatra of the tawny front? She tired of their foolishness and, leaving the chamber, found herself in a darkened hallway with young Nicholas before her.

'I did not see you weep at my death.'

'No.'

'Did I play the scene so badly?'

'I saw you weep. You played it excellently.'

'And the words I spoke, did you understand them all? Egyptian puppet?'

'Perhaps not all. I could listen to your words for hours.'

'I have forgotten them already. To me, they are a part of yesterday. Now I must learn those I will speak tomorrow. Look . . . '

From a trunk he took a painted head with drooping ears.

'Tomorrow I shall be a queen enamoured of a boor with an ass's head.'

'Tomorrow I shall not come.'

'I shall give you a gift, that you might remember today.'

Nicko unbuttoned the beaded bodice of the queen in which the asp still nestled, with its broidered tongue and eyes of glass, he handed it to her, kissed her twice and, with a bound, vanished into the dressing chamber while Margaret, clutching the serpent, walked back towards the river which, at this hour, raged enough to sweep away the body of a desperate lover. Before she crossed the bridge, she tossed the snake of rags and tatters upon the waters, where it floated, following the current, and disappeared into the darkness.

THE GLASS WOMAN

Deborah Levy

The year is 1849 and yet your lips will not be so very different from my lips and the revolutions in your century will not be so different from ours but now I must take a breath as you must too and with this breath which I still have not taken I will speak to you from where I am now which is Bavaria.

Bavaria 1849.

I am observing a young woman of 23 years in age.

She is an aristocrat. I am a physician.

I am observing the catastrophic poetry of her body.

The month is August, it is past midnight and she is walking sideways with great difficulty down the corridors of the royal palace, her arms stretched in front of her as if she is afraid she will fall. Her green eyes are wide open as she makes her way to her chamber.

Something is wrong with Princess Alexandra Amelie.

*

On 14 July she demanded that all the furniture in the palace be covered in soft velvet and that no person should be seated next to her at the dining table, not on the right nor the left, and she announced she would no longer be able to ride her horse and that if she was to travel in a carriage it must first be lined with straw. When questioned by her royal parents the princess finally confessed that when she was a child she had swallowed a grand piano made from glass. Consequently, because of her imagined shape and fragility, she is fearful that if she knocks into anything at all or trips over her skirts or if one of the royal dogs jumps into her lap, the glass piano inside her might shatter and she will become a terrifying tangle of flesh and glass.

I was promptly summoned to the palace and consented to her anxious father's demand for my discretion in this matter. My task as physician was to remove the glass piano from her belly. He would pay me by the day for one month. If his daughter was not cured by its end she would indeed be hidden in a straw-lined carriage and taken to a convent in the black forest where she would grow old with the nuns.

Why did I agree to the impossibility of this task? It is true that I am Europe's expert on delusions of this kind and speak nine languages but I knew I would not cure her. All the same, I did not want the young princess to be persecuted or injured for inventing a language that is beyond the reach of our minds.

I have made many notes over the month. They are all useless.

She eats very little because of her imagined size.

Two spoonfuls of clear soup.

Her instructions to the servants are always very clear, perhaps as transparent as the piano inside her.

'No one must ever touch me. The clocks and porcelain must be removed from my chamber. When I walk through the palace I request my maid opens all the joining doors so I will not be crushed between them.'

The piano is a sculpture made from pain.

It has form.

It is a thought.

It is a form of thinking.

Yet she will not speak her mind.

I have seen her pick elderberries off the trees in the palace gardens and slip them into her mouth.

She arranges the red berries on her tongue and encourages the birds to swoop and catch them.

She is playful with the birds.

The piano inside her is an instrument of communication.

And so is her tongue.

She has given her tongue to the birds and her belly to the piano.

I have been observing her for twenty-eight days now and have not yet succeeded in removing the glass piano from her mind. She has grown to trust me and perhaps even welcome my company.

Why have I not disclosed to her that I have been dismissed by her parents and tonight is our last conversation?

I fear the news will break her. The cook agrees with me on this matter. I understood from the start that rational argument is powerless to remove a delusion and that I would have to employ other methods. They have all failed.

I have no other methods.

Princess Alexandra Amelie can clearly see that I am standing in my overcoat in the corridors of the palace. I have chosen not to hide in the shadows or to conceal my presence. I am waving to her now as she painfully, slowly walks towards me. In my left hand I hold the glass of aromatic wine that was given to me by the cook who has instructed my valet to pack my bags and organise my carriage for the long journey to Naples in the morning.

Alexandra Amelie is wearing a white dress, her dark hair is pinned up and her satin slippers are tied with white silk ribbons that have been knotted by her staff to ensure they will never come undone. The knotting of her ribbons alone takes two hours of her day.

'I have come to say good night, Amelie.'

'You have rain on your coat,' she says, leaning the palm of her hand against the wall to steady herself. 'Where have you been?'

'I have just returned from consoling the baker who believes he is made from butter. He will not go near his oven for fear his body turns to liquid.'

'Oh,' she says, 'and how will he sleep tonight?'

'He will strip naked and cover himself with bay leaves to keep himself cool.'

'Will the leaves give him peace of mind?'

'Yes,' I reply, 'I think they will. And you, how will you sleep tonight?'

'How I always sleep.'

'And how do you always sleep?'

'I have pierced the mattress and will cover my body with its feathers. The nights are not a problem for me.'

'I am pleased to hear that, Amelie.'

She and I have agreed to address each other informally, mostly because she does not have the breath to say my full first name, nor I her full first name and I do not wish her to call me Doctor.

I know her sleep is full of torment. She has pierced the surface of her silken pillow with a needle.

I have observed that her own breathing is shallow. It is as if the pillow is doing the breathing for her.

'My dreams are full of animals,' she says. 'They are sleepy and wounded. They lie in cribs as if babies. They moan a little.'

'What kind of animals?'

'Yesterday I watched a foal being born in the stables. The farmer pulled it out of the mare. I would not like you to pull my piano out of me like that.'

I nod and sip the aromatic wine.

'Of course, Amelie. We cannot remove your piano as if it were a tooth. When I was a younger man I sold my meat-eating teeth to fund my medical studies. I still lament the gap in my mouth which I have not chosen to fill with porcelain. A tooth is as valuable as a jewel and so is your piano.'

She laughs. It is a rasping sound, like a tear in a stretch of fabric. She tells me she has given her maid permission to travel home to visit her mother. Therefore she is walking with extra caution to her chamber.

'Your piano is a phantom of your mind,' I insist, for a physician must never be complicit with a delusion.

'No it is not a phantom.' Her fingers fleetingly touch the silken folds of her dress under which she no longer wears a corset.

'You might be right,' I reply. 'But it is not very likely.'

And what else was happening in Europe while I sipped fine wine in the lavish corridors of the royal palace? The potato crop had been destroyed by a blight and suffering peasants everywhere were plotting to overthrow the feudal system.

'Just one last question.' Princess Alexandra Amelie touches her left eyelid with the tip of her soft finger. 'What will you be doing when you return to your lodgings tonight?'

'I will sit by the fire and think about you.'

'Good night Tomas.'

'Good night Amelie.'

Yet we do not move. The palm of her right hand still rests on the wall that is covered in a tempest of gold leaf.

'Just one last question,' I say. 'How will you unknot your shoes if you cannot bend your body and your maid is visiting her mother?'

'I will sleep in my shoes tonight.'

She smiles and continues on her way.

At the beginning of her treatment I witnessed a conversation that took place with my patient and her parents. Her mother had cried in exasperation.

'Alexandra Amelie what has got into you?'

'A grand glass piano, that's what,' her daughter replied.

Her parents, fearing their daughter had exchanged her sanity for a glass phantom, requested that I perform surgery and cut the piano out of her stomach.

It was a strange idea yet it helped me understand that if they imagined it could be taken out of her in this manner, it was possible for the princess to imagine it had entered her in the first place.

In the second week I noted she pierced a lemon with thorns from a rose bush.

I asked her if it was a magic object.

'Oh no. It is to release the scent of the lemon.'

She later told the cook (who has an alluring mole above her lip) that I was insane.

The surgeon's knife is not as crucial an instrument for understanding human consciousness as the imagination. Does Alexandra Amelie know her parents departed two days ago to meet the abbess of the convent and inspect their daughter's room?

I was not lying to my patient when I told her about the sad demented baker who believes he is made from butter. Here in melancholy Bavaria I have become used to the grey skies and rain. I do most of my thinking in a mustard bath at the end of a long useless day. I am thirty-six years of age and have encountered many glass delusions on my travels, yet this is my first glass piano. A philosophy professor in Rome believed he was trapped in a glass bottle. A French king believed his whole body was made from glass and wore iron ribs over his clothing to protect him if he should fall. There are men who believe their buttocks are made from glass and refuse to sit down. There have been reports throughout Europe of glass bones, hearts, chests and fingers. A carpenter from Venice refused to leave his house in case he was used by a glazier to make a window. Another glass man would only walk in the middle of the road for fear a tile from a roof would fall on his head.

So far there are no records of women who suffer from glass delusions.

In the third week I had suggested she wrap her piano in a soft warm blanket. It was a conceptual exercise. I thought it might give her some protection from her fear of breaking but she refused to accept my language. Despite her physical frailty she likes her piano naked and told me, gently, that the idea of a blanket offering her protection was a delusion.

Her father is right. I have failed to break into her body which is also her mind.

Tonight the atmosphere in the palace corridors is serene as the princess performs her strange sideways walk. The absence of her parents is a liberation. Downstairs, the staff are drinking in the kitchens and the cook is discussing with the gardener the story of Oedipus, as told by Sophocles in his tragic play, *Oedipus Rex*.

Alexandra Amelie is slim and poised but in her mind she is as wide as a grand piano.

She points to the small lion made from stone that lies on a marble slab to the left of the corridor.

'I used to sit astride it when I was a child,' she says in her low trembling voice. 'I had to lift up my petticoats and sometimes I told it to run away with me from the palace.'

'Is the past hidden in your piano Amelie?'

'Oh no.'

We can hear the cook and the gardener shouting at each other in a rage. The cook has raised her voice to insist that when Oedipus plucked out his eyes it did not stop his mind from seeing whatever it was that had distressed him in the first place.

'Alexandra Amelie, it has stopped raining and the night is warm. Let us walk to the lake and watch the swans.'

'If you have the patience, Tomas. It will take a long time to get there.'

I do have the patience.

I ask the staff to carry soft fabrics and silken cushions to the bench that is situated on the edge of the lake. I demand they light candles and bring out more wine from the cellar. And I request a plate of kaiser rolls and a bowl of fruit.

It takes three hours to walk with her to the lake in the palace gardens.

It is not far and if I was alone it would take me no longer than twelve minutes. Even a small snail is a hazard to the princess. If she were to trip or lose her balance it would be a disaster. I can guess that she has mapped an image of her body onto the surface of her brain and it includes the grand piano made from glass. She is a giant to herself. She believes she has changed shape and size. Her veins are prominent because her skin is pale, she is blue-blooded as they say of aristocrats. Alexandra Amelie avoids the sun in case the piano inside her absorbs its heat and cracks.

It suits her to be walking in the gardens of the palace under the moon at three in the morning.

She is seated now on the many silk cushions arranged on the bench. I place myself at some distance from her as usual. The swans rest their heads on their wings and glide in their sleep across the silver lake. When I tell the princess their bodies are mostly hollow, that swans are filled with air, she laughs as if she is indulging a flippant fancy of my own.

The table is laid with wine and kaiser rolls that have been sprinkled with buttermilk pumpkin seeds. The cook has tempted us with other treats too. We gaze at the feast on the table.

A soufflé
Mild and sweet almonds
Strudel dusted with white powder
Fruit
A plate of torn pancakes.

*

I unpeel the rough skin of a litchi from southern China. Suddenly my fingers are wet from the soft floral flesh inside it.

I pass it to her and she holds it in her fingers.

The lake is still and deep.

'The good thing about a conversation at night is that you cannot see my face,' she whispers.

This is true.

I have noted that when she is forced to sit at the dining table she always positions herself behind a large vase of flowers so that no one will stare at her.

A nightingale is singing in one of the damp trees.

'Amelie, what does the piano add to your existence?'

'It gives it another dimension,' she says.

'If you swallowed your piano, it must taste of something.'

'It tastes like glass.'

'How does glass taste?'

'You will have to find out for yourself.'

I lift the glass of wine to my lips.

While the nightingale sings I lick the glass.

'It tastes like sand.'

'Yes,' she agrees. 'Cold sand.'

I dip my finger into the wine and rub the rim of the glass. It makes a high-pitched melancholy sound, not unlike the nightingale.

'Listen Amelie' – I lean towards her as my finger

circles the glass – 'an object that should not be alive is talking to me.'

She slumps into the velvet drapes and stares at the swans. If she were to play her glass piano, what kind of sound would it make? I suspect she will not allow it to speak to her because she fears that if she expresses herself it will shatter. She will be filled with crushed glass and then she is done for.

The swans lift their necks as the glass sings across the lake. In the ghostly moonlight they too could be phantoms, white-feathered serpents conjured by my mind.

'Where has all your life gone Amelie?'

'Into my piano.'

'But is your piano mute?'

'Oh no,' she replies, 'and anyway, why should I tell you what it says?'

She is certain that it is there. She will not be shifted from this certainty.

It is a delusion but it is also metamorphosis.

So far its significance eludes me.

'Is your piano your friend or enemy?'

'It is a torment,' she says.

As she sucks the sweet flesh of the litchi, I ask her about the first toys she played with as a child.

She tells me her father forbade toys and so she made a tortoise from mud.

'And did you hope the tortoise might take you away from the palace like the lion?'

'No, a tortoise is too slow.'

'What is there to live for, Amelie?'

'I could never tell you that.'

'Your piano could speak for you.'

'Oh it does,' she says, 'but let me ask you that same question. What is there to live for?'

It is of course the oldest question but when set upon myself it feels like a snarling dog tearing at my leg with its teeth. What is there to live for? I am aware that my colleagues might insist they live for their children or their wives or to meet once again a true love who slipped through time or to become wealthy or do some good in the world or to deepen their knowledge or witness the changing seasons or to meet strangers and step into new cultures but it is a greedy question and so I tell her the truth.

'Amelie, I do not know what there is to live for except to understand more about the mystery of your glass piano and why the baker thinks he is made from butter.'

'Yes,' she says. 'Would I be less interesting to you without the piano?'

'It is a possibility. And yet, I think you could take a chance.'

'Why would I take it?'

I fill my wine glass to the brim.

'Because without the piano you could run away from the palace.'

'I see,' she says.

'Yes Amelie,' I continue. 'Without your piano you can take some risks.'

Again I dip my finger in the cool aromatic wine and press it lightly around the border of the glass which is made from finest crystal. Its lament sounds both angelic and devilish, it is piercing and yet it is also calm.

'Does your piano have a different sort of morality from your own?'

'Yes.'

'Does it have desires that are forbidden to you?'

'I am fearful of making contact with my piano. If I was to touch it with my hands as you are touching that glass, my fingers would become damp and I'd feel nauseous.'

'Yet, if the piano has a different morality from your own, it can speak on your behalf. That is what art is for.'

We conversed in this way for a while and I suggested she make an alliance with the cook who would help her escape from the palace if she could find a way of removing the obstacle of the piano. I must have fallen asleep because when I opened my eyes it was dawn and I glimpsed her standing by the edge of the lake. At first

I thought she might throw her body into the deep dark water to end her torment. And then she stretched her arms above her head, slowly, lightly, so as not to break the piano inside her but enough to open her chest and feel the piano move. She started to speak. I heard her voice as I have never heard it before. It was deep and it was hard and it was clear as glass.

I made my way to the edge of the lake. When I was standing by her side she was still speaking.

'Tomas, the question is not how am I going to live without my piano, it is how am I going to live without you. I have wanted to keep you by my side at all times but now that I have spoken I know you will leave.'

It is true that when love is spoken out loud it can sometimes be the end or the beginning it is a circle like breath and time and the horizon which is not a straight line. We make our phantoms in every century and if encouraged it is possible they can speak for us but it is better if we can speak for ourselves. I am a traitor to love but an honourable physician.

When my carriage pulled up outside the palace gates at dawn, I told her I would be leaving for Naples.

THE ANTHOLOGY MASSACRE

Rhidian Brook

This morning I posted twelve manuscripts, at a cost of £165, to the finest publishers in the land. If it's a large amount to spend on postage, it's a small price to pay to change the literary landscape. For with *Rocinante* I believe I have achieved a kind of perfection that contemporary practitioners of the long form can only dream of achieving: a work lofty in subject matter, novel in plot, elegant in language, clever in construction, entertaining in its episodes. Academics, booksellers, reviewers, librarians and curriculum-setters will undoubtedly have to invent an entirely new category for The Work. Sending them second-class left me with enough to purchase a nice bottle of wine with which to celebrate The Launch. It was a mid-priced Rioja (*naturalmente!*), reduced from £12 to £6, and its dusty tang temporarily transported me to Spain, where I spent many months capturing the tastes, sounds and smells that give the work the veracity that all fine art requires, that textural detail that separates the real writer from the phoney. Making a horse my narrator was a challenge (I spent a day sniffing dung in Toledo

and believe me, it does not smell the same in Spain).
Sustaining that voice over 1,837 pages of double-spaced
A4 took dedication, but once I had put myself in his four
shoes I was off. I believe the great man himself would
enjoy my equine take on his most famous work and he'd
probably be annoyed for not thinking of it first. Not that
it is homage (I hear myself telling Jim McGuff on *Book
Worm*). I have been scrupulous in avoiding pastiche and
parody – two literary forms I detest – and focused on
creating a work that stands in a green field of its own.

A mile from here, a noisier if less-significant launch
is taking place in the Shard's hubristically named Zenith
Skybar, where the phonies of the contemporary literary
order have gathered and, like aristocrats of the ancien
régime, will be gorging on cheese and wine paid for by
the 'King of Letters', AC Carruthers, completely unaware
that their world is about to fall in. Yes, this country's
'twelve finest writers' are tonight congratulating themselves on the launch of their dubiously conceived and
pretentiously named *The Anthology*, a collection of short
stories celebrating the four hundredth anniversary of the
death of Cervantes, who will no doubt be turning in his
recently located unmarked grave. I have visited the Shard
many times and I can safely say that it is a fitting venue
for such a self-congratulatory event. We live in a world
of endless up-puffery, where the most ordinary mediocrities – footballers, video artists, AC Carruthers – are
declared 'genius' and then put on pedestals, from which

unearned elevated positions they look down and assume they've done something that sets them above the rest of us. I can see them now, getting giddy on the view and their collective back-slappery: AC Carruthers in his signature white linen suit and panama, a look as studied and dated as his fungal prose, telling everyone that *The Anthology* was his idea. Declan Magee, who is thought to have some magical facility for storytelling by dint of being Irish. Vikram Bat adopting the faux wisdom and cod humility of the successful outsider. Brianny de Havilland (there because of her overwrought and over-praised second novel *When The Sun* (a title that inevitably leads a reader to ask: 'When the sun what?')). She'll be trying oh-so-hard not to show how excited she is to be among such company. Especially when that company includes her mentor, Esther Speranza, who described *When The Sun* as 'a soaring triumph' and whose own 'artistic freedom' led her to do away with punctuation, an affectation that renders it impossible to read her work without wanting to kill yourself – or her.

I have no desire to be among such company but, were I there, I would clearly not be out of place. My intimate familiarity with the Spanish master (for whom I feel an affinity more deeply than any of the chancers quaffing cava in the thousand-foot finger) would be reason enough; but I am also more than a match for any of them when it comes to the short form. They resemble long-distance runners competing in a sprint event, wholly unsuited to the requirements of that most exacting medium; a medium for which I received one of the highest accolades, when my story – 'Sirens In The Night' – was runner-up at the Bideford Story Festival (a kind of Nobel of the shorter form), an achievement for which I received a cheque for £50 and the recognition of the literary world. For the judge that day was none other than publisher Stanley Wilson, spotter of nascent literary talent, whose encouraging words provided the catalyst I needed to grow *Rocinante* from humble seed to game-changing tome.

A few years after my breakthrough at Bideford, I met Stanley at a festival at which AC Carruthers was promoting his latest 'already-optioned-for-film' drivel. Stanley was patiently listening (as we all must) to the unnecessarily initialled Carruthers (isn't Anthony Carruthers distinctive enough?). Carruthers was rocking on his heels with the confidence of a man with three million books sold and two Hollywood adaptations under his belt. Bullish with the warm – but free – Pinot and with a prestigious literary accolade of my own, I strolled up to them with the swagger of an equal.

ME: Stanley? (It felt natural to use his first name owing to the intimate connection we had already established at Bideford (for is not a man's prose more revealing than his very person?).)

STANLEY: Yes . . . sorry . . . we've met?

ME: Donald Keyworth. Bideford. 2009. I was a winner and you were the judge. 'Sirens In The Night.'

STANLEY: Ah yes. Bideford. Lovely festival. (*Turning to AC.*) Donald. You know the novelist Anthony Carruthers?

ME: I'm familiar with your oeuvre.

CARRUTHERS: (*Clearly drunk.*) You'll get oeuvre it.

ME: (*To Stanley.*) I just wanted to thank you for encouraging me to write a novel.

CARRUTHERS: Not another one. Don't encourage him, Stanley! There's enough competition out there as it is.

ME: (*Ignoring Carruthers.*) It's *Don Quixote* told from the point of view of his horse.

STANLEY: (*Smiling, intrigued, beguiled even.*)

CARRUTHERS: Didn't Cervantes already do that? That dialogue between dogs.

ME: (*To the drunk.*) That was dogs. This is a horse. That was a short story. This is a novel. It's . . . a little more ambitious. (*To my potential future publisher.*) I was hoping I might be able to send it to you. When it's done.

STANLEY: (*Reaching for and handing me his card.*) Get in touch when it's ready. By all means.

ME: By all means, I will. I aim to have it ready for the four hundredth anniversary of the death of Cervantes. 2016.

CARRUTHERS: Didn't the Bard cop it the same year?

STANLEY: He did.

ME: Perhaps we should do something to mark the moment. Some kind of tribute. Ask the country's finest writers to submit a Cervantes-inspired story.

I'd be happy to contribute of course.

STANLEY: (*Knowing look at Carruthers.*) Interesting idea. Anthony?

CARRUTHERS: (*Conspiratorially, to me.*) Look . . . Mr . . .

ME: Keyworth.

CARRUTHERS: Want to know the best way to get published?

ME: . . .

CARRUTHERS: Take out the competition.

There have been more than the usual amount of sirens wailing this evening. But it's not this that's keeping me awake. No. It's the thought of the literary bomb that is about to go off and the changed cultural topography created by its aftermath. In his *Ars Poetica* Horace said that a work should not be published until ten years after it has been completed; but he wasn't living in an age dominated by competent, inoffensive novels with redemptive endings. I say give the people what they so desperately need. For too long the public have been held hostage by a dozen or so writers (we know who they are) who have monopolised accolades and attention and kept the rest of us at the gates asking for bread. But this is about to change. Sometimes it only takes one person – a Robespierre, a Martin Luther, a Martin Luther King – to turn over the existing order, and I don't think it far-fetched to suggest that Donald Keyworth will be a name forever associated with the overthrow to come. As I lie here, pondering these things, the dissonant sounds of police car, helicopter, fire engine and ambulance are no longer a shrill Symphony of Emergency but a harmonious orchestra playing a coronation fanfare to the new King of Letters.

When I woke this morning the 7.10 train rumbled by, two dogs barked, and there was the usual susurrus of traffic; but I knew this would be no ordinary day. When I turned on the radio the newsreader was halfway through the following sentence: 'The much-loved novelist was among twenty-three people so far known to have died in last night's attack.' I made my breakfast in the usual way: heating porridge soaked overnight in semi-skimmed milk and adding honey and banana (for us writers, routine is a sacred thing that not even catastrophic world events should interrupt). 'It appears the terrorists targeted a book launch at which the cream of literature was gathered.' Apart from the debatable claim (and clumsy metaphor) that this was literature's cream, and leaving aside the question of whether you can gather cream, it soon became clear that the media (what, almost seven hours on?) were in a state of ignorance and confusion. With few facts to go on and no culprit(s) to blame, the commentators poured their speculative guff into the gaps, caught somewhere between hagiography and obituary. One reporter described Esther Speranza as the English Proust (a description obviously lifted from the dust jacket of her indigestible tome, *Broken*). It was just as he was declaring this to be 'literature's most grievous day' that I decided to get a newspaper.

I ran to Rama News (yes, ran, despite Dr K's explicit instruction to avoid overstimulation) and as I ran my future flashed before me with the force of prophecy: in it literature was saved by an unknown craftsman who for years had been working quietly on a masterpiece that rendered the loss of the nation's supposedly finest writers in an alleged terrorist attack academic. I was so taken with this vision I walked right past Rama News. (I often run ahead of myself. It is, as Mother used to tell me, both my strength and weakness. I see more than there is: I take an acorn and see a forest; I make a bay from a grain of sand. Such is the burden of the poet.) Sanjay greeted me with his usual quip: 'Decided to get up again, Don?' I had no breath to reply with one of my customary witticisms. Instead I stared at the plastic dispensing tower containing the papers. All (except *The Independent*) carried the same shot of the Shard's shattered top floor. And all were vying for the most memorable headline. *The Mail*: 'Bloody Wednesday' (serviceable). *The Sun*: 'Shard Attack!' (my favourite). *The Guardian*: '46 Feared Dead In London Terror Attack' (groan). *The Independent*: '16.6.16' (no photo and trying hard to establish a catchy date to summarise an atrocity. Bless.). *The Telegraph*: 'Suspected Terrorist Attack On Shard' (hasty). *The Star*: 'Bastards!' (assumptive use of plural). *The Express*: 'London Blitzed' (WW2 still sells).

'What a terrible thing,' Sanjay said, as I bought a copy of every paper. 'What have those writers done to deserve such a thing?'

Not having a television, I took myself to the pub where they show the football. There, I found two men nursing pints and craning necks, watching the plasma screen that is suspended high in the corner of the saloon. Considering this was an attack on writers they hadn't heard of who had written books they almost certainly hadn't read, they were quite agitated. I stood just behind them, keeping my distance, and watched as the television ran a moving ticker tape at the bottom of the screen announcing the latest casualty figures. The larger, more threatening gentleman had a tattoo of Shakespeare on his forearm with the inscription, 'To be or what?' He was particularly exercised by the unfolding scene.

SHAKESPEARE: Towelhead cunts. (Given the presence of Vikram Bat at the party you can forgive people for thinking the strike might be religiously motivated. Bat made a name for himself less for his tedious, singsong syntax and cod post-imperialist reflections, than for being crassly provocative by announcing that all religions including his own were 'an evil which needed to be eradicated from this earth'. I suppose he's now experienced what some people call 'bad karma'.)

SHAKESPEARE'S MATE: They don't know who did it, Jez. You can't say that. No one's claimed responsibility.

(Responsibility is a funny choice of word for these acts. Why claim responsibility? Surely it would be more effective not to accept responsibility and thus keep everyone guessing?)

The reporter started conducting one of those awful eyewitness interviews with a woman who actually said: 'There was this enormous bang and I thought: OMG, it's a bomb!'

I left just as a hapless reporter started quoting from Vikram Bat's portentous and frankly plagiaristic novel, *All Our Houses*: 'Will not our words grow like flowers from these ashes?' (Not yours, Vikram, not yours.)

Although my manuscripts will have arrived at the publishers' today I must try and be patient. They are unsolicited. (I have forgone the use of an agent after Batstone Buckley Butler rejected *Rocinante*: 'Dear Mr Keyworth, Thank you for sending us the manuscript for your novel *Rocinante's Revenge*. We admire your ambition but it is not one for us. The current climate is not favourable for publishing novels of this length', etc.) Most of the publishers will be a little distracted. Eleven of the twelve have lost a prized author in what the media are disappointingly deciding to call Bloody Wednesday. (A shame. It deserved a better moniker. Something like 'The Anthology Massacre' would have been more fitting, I think.) But publishers shouldn't be too downhearted. Sudden, dramatic death can lead to increased sales. *The Anthology* is No. 2 on Amazon, kept from the No. 1 slot by Florence Peters' book on cooking everything in butter. Works of the recently deceased writers make up positions 5, 8, 9, 12, 13, 55, 60, 78, 90 and 240. Proving that 'The soldier shows to greater advantage dead in battle than alive in flight.'

Esther Speranza got the first obituary. In homage to her, the obituary was written without punctuation. As with her novels, I gave up reading halfway through. Carruthers was given half the culture section in the *Sunday Times*, which used the unfortunate phrase 'body of work'. Thoughtless, given what an explosion does to the body. And it was only a matter of time before some buffoon had to describe the bombing as 'Literature's Munich'. A terrible analogy. Writers are hardly team players and tend to show murderous envy towards their fellow practitioners. See Cranson's demolition of Carruthers' last novel in the *LRB*, which I can recall word for word: 'With his every sentence straining for greatness Carruthers seems to be suffering from a particularly chronic form of literary piles: his prose purple, bulbous, irritating.' There were three more obits: William Woolwich, the spy writer who thought his work should be on the school curriculum, got an indulgent 82 lines. McGee (140 lines!) was described as 'a voice of a generation'. (Not mine.) Even that God-bothering token Welshman, Rhidian Brook, got 50 lines. I watched a *Late Show* discussion in which they tried (and failed) to assess 'the loss to literature'. It was full of

Churchillian phrases à la 'We shall not see their like', etc. The presenter did manage to introduce some light into the darkness by asking who might fill the vacuum created by Bloody Wednesday. Who indeed? It is laughable (and I have laughed out loud several times) watching the media failing to give this event the perspective it needs. The facts: forty-three people have died, among them twelve writers of debatable reputation. But no, they give us: 'The Day The Words Stood Still'.

How long should you give a publisher when they (a) have recently lost their most prized author? And (b) have a masterpiece by a new author in their in tray? Having both things occur at the same time must be unprecedented so it is hard to know. But I'm getting twitchy. They are now saying the incident was 'An attack on' – variously – 'Western values', 'London', 'Democracy', and 'Everything That Is Good', but they clearly have no idea who carried it out. When asked who they think is responsible, the Chief of Police said: 'We are exploring all avenues but, rest assured, we will find the people who did this.'

The words (the ones that matter) have not stood still! Today – at the keen-to-see-me time of 5.56 a.m. – an email pinged into my inbox from Stanley Morris himself! 'Dear Mr Keyworth, thank you for the manuscript. I would like to discuss it with you. I have a number of memorial services to attend but I am free Thursday. Does

11 a.m. at my office suit? Yours, Stanley Morrison.' A quick check of my diary revealed that, apart from a morning session with Dr K, I was free. My reply was concision itself: 'Dear Stanley. I will be there. If there is anything I can bring (apart from hope), let me know. DQK.' (The Q of my middle name suddenly appearing in my sign-off was unexpected but looked somehow more authorial.)

I decided to walk to the offices of Trebazon Publishing. Walking offers up the thoughts that become poetry, steps to stanzas so to speak, and I am already thinking of The Next Thing. My follow-up to *Rocinante*. It will be a hard act to follow, I know, but necessary for the building of my oeuvre. London seemed quieter than usual. The bombing must have dissuaded a few more tourists from visiting (another plus). As I walked I imagined myself to be last writer in the country (which, in a sense, I am); a knight answering the call of his mistress in distress. That mistress being Literature herself.

The receptionist sent me straight to Stanley's office. He limped towards me, ushering me to sit in the chair opposite his desk. The foreign editions of Carruthers' works filled half the shelves behind his desk (proof that you can be fooled in any language). I ignored the wall of ordure and focused instead on the kindly publisher. If I had to choose one person to come out of the blast unscathed it would have been Stanley Wilson. He was a lucky man (given where the device was planted). The explosion had left him with a stutter and a ringing in his ears which I reassured him would pass as the bomb was not as primitive as the devices used in World War II. Stanley's face had been cut with the shards of the Shard (a phrase I was sensitive enough not to share. Comedy is tragedy plus time as they say and two weeks was not quite enough time to make a joke, however clever, about that.). At first Stanley seemed a little subdued, but perhaps thoughtful is a better word. *Rocinante* would have given much to think about.

'Thank you for sending your n-n-novel. It's . . . ' (I could see him trying to find the right word and, unsurprisingly, struggling.) ' . . . unique. And . . . long.'

'It could probably use a . . . trim,' I said. (I wanted to show him I wasn't precious about The Work.)

'Yes.' (A pause.) 'Your covering letter was certainly the longest I have ever received.' (The Letter was thirty-two pages and a work worthy of being published in its own right (which it may well be at a later date, of course).) 'I was curious about something you said here.' (He started to read from The Letter.) '"I have always felt a deep connection with *Rocinante*: sat upon, ignored, beaten and humiliated by fools with more famous names . . . " And then you say, "The state of English letters is in p-par-parlous condition. Something needs to be done. For too long literature has been dominated by mediocrities (we all know who they are)." And then you list them.'

He put down the letter and looked at me. 'I just thought it strange that the twelve writers you mention all perished in Bloody Wednesday.'

'People say I have a gift for prescience,' I said.

He became tearful again and I took it upon myself to lift his spirits.

'Perhaps providence has kept you alive, Stanley. So that you can pass on the fictional flame to the next generation. Look, just when you have lost one of your . . . thoroughbreds' (a forced, sympathetic nod to the wall of ordure) 'Providence sends you *Rocinante* to join the Trebazon stable, as it were.'

I think this touched him because he was silent for a long, long time, nodding as if finally realising the significance of what I was saying. His silence encouraged me to be even more candid.

'I think The Anthology Massacre, as I prefer to call it, is a sort of cull, yes. A slaying of a behemoth. Literature had become a dragon. And some dragons can only be brought down by fire.'

He looked at me, open-mouthed, the way people look at you when you tell them something they know to be true but simply haven't seen.

'Of course, it is . . . a shock,' I said. 'But it is also an opportunity. Sometimes you have to clear the field to let the horse run free.'

He didn't know what to say to this. But truth needs no adorning.

How typical that the happiest day of my life coincides with an official day of mourning (they really are dragging this out). Nevertheless, while the nation shed tears over people they won't miss and can still (let's face it) read, I followed Stanley's advice and began the painstaking work of trimming *Rocinante*. It's a hard task, killing your darlings as they say. In a way, a writer's work is never done. There is always something you can improve – a comma you can remove, a bracket you can add. I've been working for ten hours and am still on page 309, which is, if I recall rightly, the exact height of the Shard in metres.

I hear sirens. Not as many as on the night that literature was changed forever. But closer, almost loud enough to be in my street. I can see lights flashing against my curtains and there are now shouts and car doors slamming. More flashing. Banging. Quite a commotion. Some petty criminal – drug dealer or pimp – chased to some hideout perhaps? Some bank robbers cornered in a last stand? Or maybe a suspected terrorist plot pre-empted. The kerfuffle is hardly conducive to creative thinking but I press on (for writers must shut out the world). And as I sit here, pen poised, the sound of many feet coming up the stairs, I suddenly realise what is going on. Stanley, unable to keep to himself the knowledge of what I have done, has tipped off the media, and the media, unable to contain its excitement, has sent its representatives to try and get the first exclusive. Yes. It's taken them a few weeks, but it seems the identity of the man who put a bomb under literature will soon be revealed to the world.

SHAKESPEARE, NEW MEXICO

Valeria Luiselli
translated by Christina MacSweeney

'When will we get there?' the children asked.

'How much longer?' they insisted.

It's always the same. The car doors close and the boys have to ask for some kind of confirmation that the journey will eventually end. I told them it was just two more hours, that we'd arrive in the late afternoon. I don't think they are ever really interested in the reply, though. I imagine those particular questions are a protest, nothing more. A protest just for the sake of it.

But maybe they are also a way of telling us they won't put up with having to look at our backs, won't tolerate us not looking at them. It undoubtedly unsettles them to be able to see only the crowns of our heads over the high front seats: my lopsided bun, like something a superannuated samurai might have; my husband's thinning black waves. From behind, we can't have been a very inspiring sight. An ordinary man and an ordinary woman, former dancers with the Ballet Folklórico Mexicano de Chicago. Two people – who happen to be their parents – resigned to following the straight line of the highway with the same docility they confront everything else in life.

At times, as we progressed through this enormous country, their father told them stories – also thinning and wavy, uninspiring. When it was my turn to provide some entertainment, I didn't tell them any stories because I don't know how. Instead, I set them riddles I'd learned so many lives ago that I couldn't even remember the answers:

A cowboy goes into a saloon. He's soaked through. He asks for a glass of water, and the bartender hands him a pistol. Then, the cowboy says 'Thank you' and leaves the saloon.

'That's it?' asked the eldest.

'That's it,' I confirmed.

'That's the end of the story?' said the little one.

'Yes, my love, that's the end of the riddle,' I said.

'Is it important to know that he's soaked, Mom?' asked the eldest.

'Yes it is.'

'Was he really soaked, Ma?' checked the youngest.

'No, I didn't say he was really soaked. But he was at least wet.'

'OK,' they both said, and began a long deliberation about the cowboy, the glass of water and the pistol, until their thoughts strayed and developed into a game with rules so arbitrary and capricious, they were impossible to understand or follow from the front seats. Just as so often before, the game gradually turned into a debate about the rules of playing it. The boys argued until sleep unravelled them. In the car, they both sleep with their mouths open, their heads hanging to one side, or drooping forwards, always in positions that give them a sinister similarity to dead bodies. They only woke when we finally pulled over at the entrance to the town.

Right from the start, we discovered a rule for getting through the slow, laborious trek from the Midwest to the Southwest of this country: we had to lie to the boys. If we generated high expectations about the place where we were going to spend the following months – telling them exaggerated, even false stories about it – the whole thing would be much more bearable for them and, consequently, for us too. It didn't matter that, afterwards, reality would completely betray those expectations. Anyway, we thought, disappointments are character-forming. The boys needed that, because what awaited them was not an easy life. It was a tolerable, perhaps even interesting life, but not easy. They were going from being little Chinelo dancers in the Ballet Folklórico in Chicago to being real actors in the American West.

Our auditions for the Southwestern Re-enactment Company had begun two years earlier. We were in the changing room of a high school in downtown Chicago, where the four of us had gone to dance with our company, and had seen several of the flyers pasted on the walls: the Southwestern Re-enactment Company was looking for families willing to move to New Mexico or Arizona, no previous acting experience required, and the age range was from four to sixty-five. A phone call to the number provided filled in the rest of the details: the auditions were to be held during the last week of March in the State Auditorium in Tucson, the scene to be performed would last at most three minutes, and participants would be notified of the results by email on the Sunday evening, that same weekend, the last weekend in March. If we were selected, our contracts would start on 1 June.

My husband had been more enthusiastic than me about the prospect of moving to the Southwest to work as actors for a historical re-enactment company. He was tired of dancing Huapangos and Jarabes, and thought that, at least for our children's sake, we had to assimilate better into the United States. It was about time we did, he said. Besides, we had to stop representing something that even in Mexico was considered foreign.

I had my doubts about the change. My only experience of acting had been humiliating. At the age of twelve or thirteen, I'd memorised Macbeth's soliloquy after Lady Macbeth's death, when the English soldiers, guided by Malcolm, are about to enter the castle to oust and kill the unlawful king – Tomorrow, and tomorrow, and so on. When I auditioned for Macbeth's role, my drama teacher had congratulated me on my good memory and fine diction, but afterwards suggested I take the role of a tree. The trees were important, she'd said: they were not actually trees but soldiers in disguise, covered in branches and leaves to intimidate Macbeth and finally drive him mad. In that production, the trees would actually be seen advancing from Birnam Wood to Dunsinane during the traitor's last hours.

But the trees didn't speak a single line and that bothered me. Gathering up my dignity, I'd refused the offer, and never again trod the boards as an actor. Instead, I'd spent my whole life representing the traditional parts of China Poblana, Jarocha, Indian Woman and even an Adelita in folkloric Mexican dances, and had never opened my mouth on stage, except to brighten up the tapping of my heels with a polite smile.

In March, as we'd planned, the four of us flew from Chicago O'Hare to Tucson, via Phoenix. We auditioned for the roles of Billy the Kid, Wyatt Earp, Big Nose Kate and Doc Holliday. They didn't hire us.

In the email turning down our application, they gently informed us that, considering we were Mexicans, it was recommendable to audition for Mexican parts rather than those we'd originally selected. My husband and I talked it over, and agreed that we could perhaps start out as Mexicans and little by little make our way up to more important roles.

The second time around, in March the following year, we were better prepared. We'd researched the history of the region, and watched new and classic Westerns. *Stagecoach* was our favourite. We'd studied a few film scripts and plays featuring Mexican outlaws and Mexican families, memorising scenes and immersing ourselves in the gestures, accents and way of life of the old Southwest. We fell in love with it all, if somewhat vicariously.

In the end, I don't know if any of that preparation was necessary. The only thing my two boys had to do in their audition was beg for money in a mock-up of a railroad station where a gunfight later took place. For my part, I was just asked to lean out an imaginary window and shout 'Juan'. I did it pretty well, considering I only had five seconds to be convincing. My husband had the scene requiring the most dramatic skill. It was the re-enactment of a confrontation that had originally taken place in 1879 between a Mexican outlaw and the legendary sheriff of Cochise, Arizona. After the sheriff had pulled out his gun and fired at point-blank range, came the following dialogue:

Sheriff: You gonna do somethin' or just lie there and bleed to death?

(*Mexican Outlaw bleeds to death.*)

Sheriff: No, I didn't think so.

This time, the email arrived a few days late, on the Wednesday night, when we were already back in Illinois and had perhaps lost hope. We were delighted to discover that, of the three Mexican families who had auditioned, we'd been selected. We were less delighted to discover that we had been assigned roles not in Tombstone, Arizona – a more settled community with a long tradition of historical re-enactments – but in the town of Shakespeare, New Mexico: a small, godforsaken place outside of Lordsburg, where a minuscule cabin and a combined salary of twenty thousand dollars for the whole season awaited us.

But the decision had been taken. When I phoned my mother to tell her we were going to live in Shakespeare, and would spend six months there – June to December – she expressed very little interest in my impassioned explanation about what it meant to be a historical re-enactor, and simply said:

'And don't get it into your head that I'll visit you there. Those places are full of pale-faced murderers.'

Her scepticism didn't touch me. Filled with enthusiasm for the life ahead, I packed the few belongings we would take with us, and we hauled them along to the other side of the country.

Between 1870 and 1890 – when the real-life events we would re-enact had occurred – there were around twenty Mexicans in Shakespeare, all miners, labourers or domestic servants. We, as a family, would represent the Bacas: Juan Baca (35), Juana Baca (28), Teresio Baca (6) and Victor

Baca (4). As there were more male roles in the town than available actors, my husband Juan Baca would also play, as required, Mexican Outlaw, Mexican Smuggler and Mexican Bandit, just so long as those parts didn't coincide with his scenes as Juan Baca, a peon with more duties and a higher status than any other Mexican in town.

Shakespeare had been founded in 1856, and was later re-founded several times with equal lack of success. In 1879, there was a small mining boom, but the town never expanded enough to warrant the construction of either a school or a church. When the railroad that entwined the country in a single, powerful commercial route was finally built, the nearest station ended up being three whole miles away, in Lordsburg, and this fact buried the town of Shakespeare in the dust. The last of its residents left in about 1893.

Years later, in 1935, Frank and Rita Hill bought the abandoned town, or what remained of it. They set up a ranch, and when that went bust, they transformed it into the rickety site of historical re-enactments we were now driving into. With the passing of the last generation of the Hill family, which had – again, with no great success – carried on the traditions of the town and its re-enactments, the company in Tucson that had held the auditions purchased the concession, with the intention of making maximum profit at minimum cost.

That was the story of Shakespeare, at least in the version delivered to us by a lame and taciturn Doc Holliday, whom we met at the entrance to Shakespeare upon our arrival. Very soon, he was comparing his misfortune with ours. As he was showing us to our cabin, at one end of town, he confessed that he, too, would have preferred to be Tombstone's Doc Holliday rather than Shakespeare's. He'd worked in the latter for two seasons now, and the wages weren't even enough to give his family – in California – a decent life. He was making arrangements to go back to them, and for some time now had been secretly preparing for an audition as Mickey Mouse in Disney – three times his salary as Doc Holliday. He could hardly wait to get out of Shakespeare.

We also learned from him that, in addition to earning comparatively low wages, the actors in Shakespeare worked much harder than those in Tombstone, let alone Disneyland. In order to make Shakespeare a going concern, the company managing our historical re-enactments had decided that we would offer an experience that was 'more real than real life'. In practice, that meant the actors in Shakespeare lived right there on-site, wore period costumes every day, and were permanently in character, so that when any tourists turned up in the town, they would have the impression that they were voyeurs in a real place, and not the audience in some artificial, ephemeral tourist trap.

In addition to the accurate representation of daily life in the late nineteenth century, we offered re-enactments of the seven most iconic events that had put Shakespeare on the historical map as a cowboy town: 'Just One Dia-mond', 'Death Over an Egg', 'Happy Bob Passes On', 'Lynched on the Porch', 'The Hanging of Arkansas Black', 'Silver Nuggets Visit Shakespeare' and 'Death of a Gov-ernment Contractor'. The golden rule was that these re-enactments, unlike those in any other so-called ghost town, were never scheduled. They happened spontane-ously. That's to say, when one of the actors involved in a scene pronounced a phrase or part of a speech from it, the scene in question would run from that line.

For example: 'Death Over an Egg'. If the actor who played Ross Woods in that scene walked into the Stratford Hotel one morning at about nine o'clock and told the waitress: 'Gimme an egg, why don't ya?'

Then I – usually, at that moment, cleaning the floor of the corridor behind the scene – had to run upstairs and wake Bean Belly Smith, so that he'd come straight down, still in his pyjamas, sit down at an empty table, and also order an egg. Then, he'd start cursing Ross Woods loudly and aggressively, across the room, having being told by the waitress that Woods had just ordered the last egg in the hotel kitchen.

Putting his knife and fork down on his empty plate, Ross Woods would leave his table silently, go upstairs to his room to fetch his pistol, come down again and shoot – but miss – Bean Belly Smith from the doorway. Woods would then be hit by a bullet from Smith's pistol, which would send him staggering – another stream of curses – until he fell, sometimes at the bottom of the stairs, sometimes on a table, sometimes on the floor. And so ended 'Death Over an Egg'.

After that, we could all get on with our regular tasks until some other phrase, spoken in the post office or the dry goods store, would spark off 'Just One Diamond' or 'The Hanging of Arkansas Black' or any other of the seven official re-enactment scenes. And so our days unfolded, almost always happily.

My children's favourite scene was 'Lynched on the Porch', in which the cowboys Sandy King and Russian Bill were the victims of a lynching. The re-enactment opened when our sheriff and hangman, Dangerous Dan Tucker, found out that Sandy King and Russian Bill had rustled some of his cattle. Dangerous Dan Tucker was famous for his ruthlessness, and his hatred of Apaches, Mexicans and foreign folk in general. I kept well away from him, just in case there was something of the character in the actor.

On discovering that his cattle had been stolen, Dangerous Dan Tucker organised a 'vigilance committee', composed solely of himself and his ass-licker sidekick, the bartender Jim Caroll. After the mock trial, the two of them took the cattle thieves across the street, where the nooses were strung from the porch. Before the hanging, King famously asked for a drink of water to wet his throat, which, he claimed, was dry from so much talking to save his life.

Once the two cowboys had been hanged, the four youngsters in the town – my sons Teresio and Victor Baca, the wild John Wray, son of a German miner and the waitress at the Stratford Hotel, and Nimmi, the beautiful, captive Apache girl who lived as a kind of slave with Dangerous Dan – came running out from their respective homes. They planted themselves in front of the bodies of Sandy King and Russian Bill and started to throw stones and sand at them. The kids were pitiless. Some afternoons, I watched them from my window. Backlit by the long rays of the setting sun, those four savage, insolent children looked beautiful as they laughed, and hollered, and threw golden handfuls of dirt at the two corpses dangling in the air.

In the beginning, we all used to wait diligently for the cues to our respective scenes. On some days, we even spent hours repeating the same scene over and over, dozens of times, with minor variations, in order to internalise and perfect them. But as the months passed, some actors began to tire of the routine. They perhaps despised the burdensome repetitiveness of their everyday lives, the feeling they were following a circular track that always led back to the same small, identical actions. One morning, in September, for example, the waitress at the Stratford actually stabbed poor Ross Woods with a blunt knife when, newly resurrected from his fourth straight death, he turned to her and muttered once again, 'Gimme an egg, why don't ya?'

I, however, never tired of our re-enactments. With time, I learned to love and master my scenes, putting all the devotion and care into them that our town, our Shakespeare, deserved. We were, it seemed to me, like an old-time circus troupe, except that the world came to us instead of us going to the world. Our lives were free and unconstrained: they were far away from all those castrating institutions, far from the servitude to unnecessary technology, and free from the weight of having to act as ourselves. They were far, also, from that country out there, which was always advancing on its unforgiving path toward progress and power; far from that cruel and loveless country beyond the last little shack in our town. Sincere friendships began to grow between some of the actors: my husband Juan and Doc Holliday spent almost every day together, and the Government Contractor, who lived a few houses down from us, soon joined them. Nimmi, the Apache girl – I later learned she was not Apache, but the first-generation immigrant daughter of a Tamil family, and had grown up in Tulsa, Oklahoma – started to visit me each morning. We'd drink a cup of milky coffee together and eat a slice of bread and butter in silence, while my sons were over at the corrals or cleaning out the chicken hutch in the backyard. Afterwards, she'd help me pick the grubs out of the beans and lentils, and I'd help her grind the nuts and acacia seeds we later mixed to make bread.

*

Dangerous Dan and Doc Holliday had a particularly gory confrontation with the famous Wild West malefactor Billy the Kid, who used to return to Shakespeare from time to time to torment us all. At sundown, every now and again, Billy the Kid would kick open the door of our cabin, looking for his enemy, Doc Holliday. With his thumbs tucked into his gun belt, he'd stand in the middle of our dining room, looking down on us from his short but dignified stature, interrupting our supper. Furious at not finding Doc Holliday, he'd take Juan Baca out of the cabin at gunpoint and tie him to the hitching post outside the sheriff's office, where some afternoons – if no one had got around to cutting them down – the tired bodies of Sandy King and Russian Bill were still hanging. After tying Juan Baca to the post, Billy the Kid would return to the cabin, take me hostage, march me to a room in the Stratford Hotel and rape me.

The rape, of course, didn't happen, and our scene together ended when he pushed me, or sometimes dragged me by the hair, into what served as one of our props rooms in the hotel. We had to wait ten or fifteen minutes there, after which I returned to the cabin, and he set out to look for Doc Holliday, buttoning up his fly as he went. He'd find Doc in the central square, and attempt – without success – to kill him, before galloping back towards Lordsburg in the dark, dodging the erratic gunfire of Dangerous Dan, who would have just come out of the sheriff's office, always at least a bit tipsy, his revolver in hand.

Billy the Kid carried himself with an air of calm assurance. He had a way of being distant, but didn't seem indifferent or insensible to the world. More than fearsome, he looked dangerously vulnerable, like those American teenagers who one fine day suddenly open fire on their classmates without anyone ever having expected that, or anything else, from them. He had a desert-hard face, furrowed by the sun and tobacco smoke, in which a pair of blue eyes and a gaze of almost bovine docility seemed out of place. He preferred Mexican hats to the cowboy variety, had killed his first victim at the age of seventeen, survived Apache raids, hunted buffalo and broken out of jail twice; he was an excellent dancer, had a universally disarming sense of humour, and spoke Spanish. His last words, in fact, were spoken in that language: on 14 July 1881, in the dark kitchen in which his murderer was waiting for him, he asked, '*Quién es, quién es?*' before receiving a fatal shot in the chest. Of all the characters in Shakespeare, Billy the Kid was undoubtedly the most complex, the saddest, and something in his blue eyes silently pleaded for salvation.

The dry, rasping heat of summer passed and the redeeming October winds began to blow. There was just under three months left to the end of the season. Nimmi, the false Apache girl, was by then spending the whole day

223

with me in the cabin, as far as possible from Dangerous Dan, whom she despised more and more with each
passing day. Ross Woods had jumped ship, fed up of the
Stratford waitress's increasingly venomous invectives.
The fainthearted Doc Holliday had still not got his much-
sought-for job offer in California – not as Mickey Mouse,
nor Shrek, nor even a pink hairy monster from a movie
only my children have seen and would remember. Every
day, for want of a better idea, Doc Holliday – abetted by
Juan Baca, and with waning resolution – would kill the
Government Contractor, who came to claim the cow we
kept in the corral behind the cabin. It was a long, dispas-
sionate shoot-out, after which the murderers dragged
their victim up a hill to the west of town, where they
dug a pit and buried him. So ended the scene 'Death of
a Government Contractor'.

A few minutes later, the murdered Contractor would
rise up from his grave, first poking his head above the
ground to check there were no tourists around to witness the change of scene. It was an unnecessary precau-
tion because hardly anyone ever visited us except lost
couples, occasional busloads of pensioners, or the odd
group of Mexican or Central American migrants who
had crossed the border at Douglas or El Paso and strayed.
Having ensured that no one was looking, the Contractor
would start off downhill to where his wagon was tethered
near the entrance to town. He'd brush the dust off his
clothes, get into the wagon, take a turn around the town,

pull up behind a clump of bushes and finally enter his house. That's where Juan and Doc Holliday would find him. Together, the three would drink the various pints of bourbon that, every night, left them lying like newly felled trees wherever they dropped.

For my part, after a few months of playing the scene with Billy the Kid, I began to await his irruption into our cabin with nervous anticipation. The afternoons when he failed to turn up, and the sun had already begun to set behind the bare hillside outside my kitchen window, seemed grey and pathetic. I resented his ever more frequent absences to the point of considering writing to the company to complain about his apparent disinterest in his work and neglect of his responsibilities. My dislike of the vile Dangerous Dan also increased, since it was his intimidations that, when you came down to it, drove Billy the Kid out of Shakespeare on the odd occasions he did appear.

I came up with a plan. It occurred to me that if, one day, with Nimmi's discreet complicity, I could manage to ensure that the lynching of Sandy King and Russian Bill preceded the irruption of Billy the Kid, and my later kidnapping, by a few minutes, and that this scene almost immediately preceded the Contractor's, I could perhaps extend my time with Billy the Kid in the Stratford Hotel long enough for us to consummate our – until then unfinished – scene together. It was a scheme more complicated than complex, but it was possible.

225

Juan Baca would be tied to the hitching post outside the sheriff's office, and the children would arrive to throw stones and dirt at Sandy King and Russian Bill. As Juan wouldn't be in the cabin when the Government Contractor came to claim our cow, his knocks on our door would receive no answer. Doc Holliday would come round the back of the cabin and, noting that Juan wasn't there, would have to run to untie him, maybe dodging the stones the children would then be throwing at the freshly lynched bodies of Sandy King and Russian Bill. Only then could the two of them – Doc Holliday and Juan – return to the cabin and get in through the back door, behind the Contractor's back. Nimmi, in the meanwhile, would be taking care of the drunken Dangerous Dan.

By that time, Billy the Kid and I would have been alone for a good while in the hotel room.

The day came in the middle of December. It was a cold but radiant afternoon. For the first time in weeks, a busload of pensioners had arrived in Shakespeare from Silver City, and their presence had us all on edge.

The sun was going down, and Juan Baca and Doc Holliday were dodging stones outside the sheriff's office. Unaccustomed to visitors, and spurred on by the applause and laughter from their audience, instead of hurrying on to the scene with the Contractor – who was already waiting for them at the cabin – they lingered there even longer than I had calculated.

Billy the Kid and I had been in the room for a few minutes, looking out the window onto the main square. To make conversation, and keep him entertained, I suggested a riddle: a cowboy goes into a saloon, he's soaked through. He asks for a glass of water, and the bartender hands him a pistol. The cowboy says 'Thank you' and leaves the saloon. Why?

Billy looked at me the way a cow would contemplate a fly circling around it and said:

'The cowboy had the hiccups. Is that the best you can do, honey?'

I raised my eyebrows: I was lost for words. A change of strategy was in order. I said I was worried that if we went out of the room straight away, it would be too early to do the scene with Doc Holliday, and he'd have to mooch around the town aimlessly, waiting for the Contractor to be buried on the hilltop. That seemed to convince him to stay put. We agreed that it wouldn't be a good idea to leave the props room until the next soporific skirmish between Juan, Doc Holliday and the Contractor had come to a close, and the burial had taken place; it would then be at least twenty or thirty minutes until Holliday would be free for the dire scene in which he and Dangerous Dan run Billy the Kid out of Shakespeare.

'What are you thinking about, Billy?' I asked.

'Eh?'

'I said what are you thinking about.'

He glanced at me out of the corner of his eye and said nothing, just turned his gaze back to the window onto the main square, where Juan Baca and Doc Holliday were basking in the heartfelt applause, doing a turn that wasn't in our script: a ridiculous routine, like something circus clowns would invent, involving acrobatics, hat throwing and shaking hands with the audience. In the meanwhile, behind them, the four children from the town – John, Nimmi, Teresio and Victor – were tying Dangerous Dan to the hitching post outside the sheriff's office. The latter must have been drunk because, instead of resisting, he went quietly along with it. We watched Nimmi slap him a couple of times, and put a heavy stone on the top of his head, forcing him to balance it there. He let it fall. She slapped him again and placed the stone back on his head. Doc Holliday then disappeared inside the sheriff's office for a few minutes and reappeared wearing a Mickey Mouse costume, firing his revolver into the air. The audience erupted into screams and roars of laughter.

Finally, Billy spoke. Without taking his eyes from the window, his face stern and expressionless, he said:

'My knife's sharp, honey.'

I wasn't sure if he meant that literally or was inciting me to do something. I thought about undoing the buttons of his waistcoat and his fly, and pulling down the long johns the men in Shakespeare wore under their woollen trousers. I'd never raped a man, much less a man of Billy the Kid's legendary proportions. Rumour had it that despite his short stature, his penis was as fat as an eggplant. The thought of it! I didn't know where to begin.

Sure that our signal to leave the room would be some time in coming, we dragged two chairs out from a corner, where they were jumbled together with a couple of brooms, a hatchet, coils of rope, a bunch of artificial flowers and a suitcase, and sat down facing each other. He lit a cigarette and I stretched one leg, allowing the side of my unshod instep to rest on his worn boot. As he didn't move an inch, I dared to slide my other foot towards him and rested it on the same boot. He watched me, maybe with indifference. I asked for a drag on his cigarette and when he held it out to me, I caught his wrist and leaned forward to put my lips to its tip. I inhaled deeply, without releasing his wrist, and fought down the desire to cough. I also fought down the suspicion that my new role as a slut was beyond my acting skills. Then, he ran a finger along the low neckline of my dress. With that gesture, I regained my confidence and sense of purpose. I stood up, pulling down the long underwear I wore under my skirt, and sat astride him, face to face. He let his cigarette fall, ground it under the sole of his boot, and put his hands around my hips.

'I'm your Huckleberry Finn,' he said. 'Why don't we have a spelling bee?'

I didn't understand the reference, or the question, but I opened his fly and ran my fingers along the stiff cloth of his long johns until I found the slit through which the tip of his penis poked, living up to its fine reputation. I gave him a long kiss that tasted of pure salt. Then I went on kissing his neck and the lobes of his ears, continuing to move my fingers between the tip of his penis and the wrinkly folds of his testicles. Outside, a gust of laughter rose from the crowd, followed by a rush of applause and whistles.

I thought that Doc Holliday and Juan Baca must finally be walking towards the cabin to meet the Government Contractor. Or perhaps the children were still holding Dangerous Dan hostage, and were playing their version of William Tell with him – instead of apples on his head, stones. Suddenly, gunshots rang out, and the erection that was just beginning to swell deflated between my hands like a burst balloon.

'Have they killed the Government Contractor?' he asked solemnly, perhaps worried.

'I don't think so,' I replied, trying to squeeze my thighs against his hips.

'Holliday's gonna catch me if I don't get to my horse on time.'

'They have to bury the Contractor first,' I said, and tried to extract his pistol, which was digging into my right thigh. He put a hand to his holster.

'I'm not afraid to die like a man, fighting, but I wouldn't like to be killed like a dog, unarmed,' he said.

I laughed, unsure if anything he said was meant to be taken seriously, or if he was really incapable of speaking to me as if we were two normal adults who are simply about to fornicate.

'You know, at least two hundred men have been killed in Lincoln County,' he went on, 'but I didn't kill all of them. People thought me bad before, but if ever I should get free, I'll let them know what bad means.'

'What?' I asked, tetchily.

'People thought me bad before, but if ever I should get free, I'll let them know what bad means,' he repeated.

'What are you saying, Billy?'

'I'm not afraid to die like a man, fighting, but I wouldn't like to be killed like a dog, unarmed,' he said again.

'Needle stuck?' I asked, standing to put my underwear back on.

'You know, at least two hundred men have been killed in Lincoln County but I didn't kill all of them,' he went on.

I walked over to the window. Billy took out his box of matches and lit another cigarette. Outside, the laughter and applause had died down. There was no one in the main square except for Dangerous Dan – still tied to the hitching post – so deeply asleep that he appeared dead, his head drooping. Nimmi was standing guard beside him, holding a shotgun. She fired twice into the wide, open sky.

I knew that was my cue. I picked up my empty chair and, in a single movement, swung it at Billy's head.

He had no time to react. A narrow trickle of blood slid down from his forehead, his whole body crumpled. His lit cigarette fell to the floor and I ground it under my bare foot.

I checked his pulse was still beating. It was. I undressed him slowly and tied him to the chair with some rope. Then I sat astride him. You could say that, in some remote sense, I danced a jig on him. When I'd finished, I put a bunch of artificial roses between his legs.

Shakespeare was silent and I'd switched off the light in the props room to be able to see, from my position on the floor, the burning desert stars.

When Billy came round, maybe forty minutes later, I was still lying face up, looking at the sky, striking and blowing out the matches he'd left by his chair when he'd lit his last cigarette. He cleared his throat and said:

'People thought me bad before, but if ever I should get free, I'll let them know what bad means.'

'Sure Billy, whatever you say,' I replied.

'You know, at least two hundred men have been killed in Lincoln County,' he went on, 'but I didn't kill all of them.'

'Shut the fuck up, Billy,' I said calmly, and he obeyed.

We went on breathing together in the darkness for a little while until we heard a slow creaking sound. The door opened, letting in the light from the hall of the Stratford Hotel. Outside, probably rather drunk, passing around a half-empty bottle, were Juan, the Contractor, and Doc Holliday, who was still dressed in his Mickey Mouse audition outfit. Behind them, like a kind of Greek chorus, a group of octogenarian tourists watched us, wide smiles on their faces, ready to enjoy the final scene their tour of Shakespeare would offer.

'*Quién es, quién es?*' murmured Billy the Kid, unable to protect himself from the flashing cameras of our audience.

I took Billy's revolver, still in the holster thrown on the floor among the tangle of his clothes. This was my moment, I was certain. I rose from the floor, and struck a match to light my face better for a few seconds. Standing next to Billy, holding his own revolver to his temple, when the flame died, I said:

> Out, out, brief candle!
> Life's but a walking shadow, a poor player
> That struts and frets his hour upon the stage
> And then is heard no more. It is a tale
> Told by an idiot, full of sound and fury,
> Signifying nothing.

Billy closed his eyes before the sound of the smoking shot was heard. He opened them again at the applause, which started slowly, timidly, and then exploded into a loud ovation. I was disappointed to discover that my children were not among the crowd watching my scene, though perhaps seeing Billy naked would have been an unnecessary shock. Juan Baca and the Contractor – arms around each other's shoulders – passed the bottle between them and, wrapped in their strange cloud of torpor and half-happiness, raised it together in a toast. The pensioners cheered and whistled with generous appreciation. Doc Holliday had taken off his white plush mitts to applaud more easily and, from behind the outsized head of his mouse costume, was shouting resounding bravos.

NOTE FROM THE EDITORS

The lunatic, the lover and the poet. What do these three have in common? According to Theseus in *A Midsummer Night's Dream*, they're 'of imagination all compact'. Those words might begin to explain the endless fascination exerted by some of Shakespeare's characters; but they seem also to be the perfect fit for an unrelated near-contemporary, providing as they do an uncannily good explanation for the hero of Cervantes's *Don Quixote*. Because Spanish literature's greatest lover-poet-lunatic is indeed compact – that is, formed – of imagination. He's not merely a product of his creator's imagining; imagination is fundamentally the material stuff out of which he is made.

A vivid imagination is what drives Don Quixote the character as much as *Don Quixote* the novel. Imagination is what supplies the answer to every 'What if . . . ?' question that sets every Shakespearean plot moving. Imagination is what takes a single original moment – a scenario, a fragment of character, a point of conflict – and over the course of thousands of words pieces out those imperfections into, well, *Henry V*, perhaps? Our twin geniuses of Alcalá de Henares and Stratford-upon-Avon not only tapped their own imaginations to create their work, but so often made that work an explicit, committed, vibrant celebration of imaginative power.

Is that, perhaps, why their stories continue to supply such rich fuel for literary creation today? Certainly the kind of imagination that constitutes and governs lunatics, lovers and poets (such as those who populate these pages) also serves to explain how the stories in this collection have come to exist. We asked a dozen brilliant novelists to take these two vast figures as their starting points and set their own imaginations to work, and far from being crippled by the anxiety of these influences, our contemporary writers acquitted themselves most bravely, launching themselves at their giants – armed only with a pen – with resourcefulness, generosity, wisdom and wit. (Just as Cervantes and Shakespeare so often did with writers who came before them, of course.) We are grateful to them, and to our twelve translators (six stories have been translated for the English edition, six for the Spanish edition) for sharing their skill and the fruits of their imaginations with us.

Some of these new stories occupy the same narrative spaces as their predecessors, but are transplanted in place or time: *Coriolanus* is moved to Mexico in Yuri Herrera's story, and Caesar and Mark Antony, who appear as both characters and literary references in Juan Gabriel Vásquez's story, to Bogotá; Mir Aslam, Kamila Shamsie's creation, is both Cide Hamete Benengeli, the fictitious narrator of *Don Quixote*, and Quixote himself, a fighter ready to face giants. Don Quixote is also the main character in Ben Okri's 'Don Quixote and the Ambiguity of Reading', which restages (and relocates) the famous visit Don Quixote makes to the printing workshop in the second book.

Some stories take merely a Shakespearean theme, or a Cervantine flavour, rather than the shape of a particular existing narrative. Cervantes's 'The Glass Graduate' remains one of his most intriguing texts and it has inspired two new stories here: Deborah Levy tells the story of Princess Alexandra Amelie of Bavaria, convinced she has swallowed a glass piano, while in 'Glass' Nell Leyshon also creates delicate characters made vulnerable by love, just like Tomás in the original story. Marco Giralt Torrente's suburban story, meanwhile, talks of the love and jealousy and treason in *Hamlet*, concealed behind layers of boring bourgeois life. And in Rhidian Brook's 'The Anthology Massacre', we find Cervantes's brutal sense of humour on every page, as an undervalued writer (much as Cervantes himself) tries to find an editor for his decidedly long novel, *Rocinante's Revenge*.

Other stories take on the real worlds of the writers that inspired them – in Vicente Molina Foix's story we meet playgoers in Jacobethan London – or that of the readers and scholars who come after them: in 'The Secret Life of Shakespeareans', by Soledad Puértolas, a story within a story leads us to a mysterious bazaar in Aleppo, while the characters recover love through boring Shakespearean lectures. In Hisham Matar's 'The Piano Bar', a man walks into a café in Cairo with a copy of *Don Quixote* under his arm. And in Valeria Luiselli's story an actor in a tacky New Mexico historical re-enactment company is really just waiting for a chance to give us a bit of her Macbeth.

In his introduction, Salman Rushdie identifies some of the possibilities modern-day storytellers have inherited from their colossal ancestors. The writers in *Lunatics, Lovers and Poets*, in embracing our challenge, have produced stories that demonstrate the richness of these possibilities; and in doing so, they open the promise of unexplored routes for those who come after them, too.

ABOUT THE CONTRIBUTORS

THE WRITERS

Rhidian Brook is an award-winning writer of fiction, television drama and film. His novels have been translated into twenty-four languages and adapted for the screen. His short stories have been broadcast on BBC Radio 4 and published in magazines including the *Paris Review*, *Time Out* and the *New Statesman*. He has also written screenplays for BBC Drama, as well as for cinema. He is a regular contributor to 'Thought for the Day' on the *Today* programme. Rhidian lives in London with his wife and two children.

Marcos Giralt Torrente has published novels, collections of short stories and a memoir. In 2014 three of his works were translated into English. In 2011 he won the Spanish National Book Award. He has received several other awards, such as the Premio Herralde in 1999 for his novel *Paris*. He was part of the DAAD Artists-in-Berlin programme in 2002.

Yuri Herrera is a Mexican novelist who won the 2003 edition of the Premio Binacional de Novela Joven with his first novel *Trabajos del reino*, which also received the Otras Voces, Otros Ambitos prize for the best novel published in Spain in 2008. His second novel, *Señales que precederán al fin del mundo* (*Signs Preceding the End of the World*), was shortlisted for the Rómulo Gallegos Prize. His work has been published in journals and newspapers in Spain, Latin America and the United States.

Deborah Levy writes fiction, plays and poetry. Her work has been staged by the Royal Shakespeare Company. Her novel *Swimming Home* was shortlisted for the 2012 Man Booker Prize, 2012 Specsavers National Book Awards and 2013 Jewish Quarterly-Wingate Prize, while the title story of *Black Vodka: ten stories* was shortlisted for the 2012 BBC International Short Story Award and another story from the collection has been turned into the graphic novel *Stardust Nation*. 'The Glass Woman' was researched at the Royal College of Art as part of Levy's AHRB research fellowship titled 'The Life of Objects: what objects tell us about our secret selves'.

Nell Leyshon is an award-winning playwright and novelist. Her first novel, *Black Dirt*, was longlisted for the Orange Prize and *The Colour of Milk* has been published worldwide. Her plays include *Comfort Me with Apples*, which won the Evening Standard Award for most promising playwright, and *Bedlam*, the first play written by a woman to be performed at Shakespeare's Globe. Nell also writes for BBC Radio 3 and 4, and her first radio play, *Milk*, won the Richard Imison Award. She taught creative writing for many years with marginalised communities, and is on the Management Committee of the Society of Authors.

Valeria Luiselli is a Mexican novelist (*Faces in the Crowd*) and essayist (*Sidewalks*) whose work has been published in the *New York Times*, the *New Yorker*, *Granta* and *McSweeney's*. In 2014, *Faces in the Crowd* was the recipient of the *Los Angeles Times* Art Seidenbaum Award for First Fiction and she was chosen as one of the National Book Foundation's '5 Under 35'.

Hisham Matar's novels, *In the Country of Men* (2006) – shortlisted for the Man Booker Prize – and *Anatomy of a Disappearance* (2011), have won several international prizes and been translated into twenty-nine languages. He is a Fellow of the Royal Society of Literature. He divides his time between London and New York, where he is the Weiss International Fellow in Literature and the Arts in the English Department at Barnard College, Columbia University. His new book, *The Return*, will be out in the summer of 2016.

Vicente Molina Foix is a Spanish dramatist, critic, and film director. His poetry was included in the famous anthology *Nueve novísimos poetas españoles* (1970), but he has mostly published novels ever since: *Busto* (Premio Barral 1973), *Los padres viudos* (Premio Azorín 1983), *La quincena soviética* (Premio Herralde 1988), *El vampiro de la calle Méjico* (Premio Alfonso García Ramos 2002). He has translated *Hamlet*, *King Lear* and *The Merchant of Venice*.

Ben Okri has published ten novels, three volumes of short stories, two books of essays and three collections of poems. His work has been translated into more than twenty-six languages. He is a Fellow of the Royal Society of Literature, honorary vice-president of English PEN and has been awarded the OBE. The recipient of many international honorary doctorates, his books have won numerous prizes, including the Commonwealth Writers' Prize for Africa, the Aga Khan Prize for Fiction, the Premio Grinzane Cavour, and the Chianti Ruffino Antico Fattore International Literary Prize. He won the Booker Prize in 1991 for *The Famished Road*. Among his credits is the screenplay for the film *N: The Madness of Reason*. He is an Honorary Fellow of Mansfield College, Oxford. Born in Nigeria, he lives in London. His latest novel, *The Age of Magic*, was published in 2014.

Soledad Puértolas won the Premio Sésamo in 1979 for her novel *El bandido doblemente armado*, the Premio Planeta in 1989 for *Queda la noche* and the Premio Anagrama de

Ensayo in 1993 with *La vida oculta*. She has published several novels, essays and stories. She has two children (one of them a writer) and lives in Madrid with her husband.

Salman Rushdie is the author of eighteen books, including *Midnight's Children*, which won the Booker Prize in 1981, the 'Booker of Bookers' in 1993, and, in 2008, the 'Best of the Booker'. *The Moor's Last Sigh* won the Whitbread Prize in 1995 and the European Union's Aristeion Prize in 1996. In 2007, Salman Rushdie was awarded a knighthood for services to literature. He is a Fellow of the Royal Society of Literature and a Commandeur de l'Ordre des Arts et des Lettres.

Kamila Shamsie is the author of six novels, including *Burnt Shadows*, which has been translated into more than twenty languages and was shortlisted for the Orange Prize for Fiction, and *A God in Every Stone* which was shortlisted for the Baileys Women's Prize for Fiction. Three of her other novels (*In the City by the Sea*, *Kartography*, *Broken Verses*) have received awards from the Pakistan Academy of Letters. A Fellow of the Royal Society of Literature, and one of *Granta*'s 'Best of Young British Novelists', she grew up in Karachi and now lives in London.

Aside from writing novels, short stories and essays, Colombian writer **Juan Gabriel Vásquez** has translated into Spanish works by EM Forster, Victor Hugo and

John Hersey. *The Sound of Things Falling* won him the 2011 Premio Alfaguara de Novela and the 2014 International IMPAC Dublin Literary Award. He has also published *The Secret History of Costaguana* (QWERTY Award), *The Informers* and *Las reputaciones* (RAE Award, 2014). His collection of stories, *The All Saints' Day Lovers*, has just been published in English.

THE TRANSLATORS

Lisa M Dillman teaches at Emory University in Atlanta, Georgia, and translates from the Spanish and Catalan. Her translations of Andrés Barba's *August, October* and Yuri Herrera's *Signs Preceding the End of the World* were published in 2015, and her translations of their next novels, *Death of a Horse* and *The Transmigration of Bodies*, respectively, are forthcoming in 2016.

Rosalind Harvey's translation of Juan Pablo Villalobos's novel *Down the Rabbit Hole* was shortlisted for the Guardian First Book Award and the Oxford-Weidenfeld Prize. Her co-translation of *Dublinesque* by Enrique Vila-Matas was shortlisted for the 2013 *Independent* Foreign Fiction Prize and longlisted for the 2014 International IMPAC Dublin Literary Award. She is founding member and chair of the Emerging Translators Network and takes part in regular translation-related events in the UK.

Anne McLean has translated Latin American and Spanish novels, short stories, memoirs and other writings by many authors, including Héctor Abad, Julio Cortázar, Ignacio Martínez de Pisón and Enrique Vila-Matas. Two of her translations have been awarded the *Independent Foreign Fiction Prize*: *Soldiers of Salamis* by Javier Cercas in 2004 and Evelio Rosero's *The Armies* in 2009. *The Sound of Things Falling*, her translation of *El ruido de las cosas al caer*, by Juan Gabriel Vásquez, won the 2014 International IMPAC Dublin Literary Award.

Christina MacSweeney's translations of works by Valeria Luiselli have been recognised by a number of literary prizes. She has also translated texts by such Latin American authors as Daniel Saldaña París, Elena Poniatowska and Silvina Ocampo. Her work has appeared on a variety of platforms, including *Granta Online*, *Words Without Borders*, *McSweeney's*, *Quarterly Conversation* and *Litro Magazine*, and in the anthology *México20* (Pushkin Press, 2015).

Samantha Schnee is the founding editor of *Words Without Borders*. Her translation of Mexican author Carmen Boullosa's *Texas: The Great Theft* (Deep Vellum, 2014) was longlisted for the International Dublin Literary Award, shortlisted for the PEN America Translation Prize and won the Typographical Era Translation Award. Her translation of Spanish author Laia Fàbregas's *Landing* will be published by HispaBooks in 2016. She is also a trustee of English PEN.

Frank Wynne is a literary translator. He has translated over fifty works by French and francophone authors including Michel Houellebecq, Boualem Sansal and Ahmadou Kourouma, and by Spanish and Latin American authors including Pablo Picasso, Tomás González and Arturo Pérez-Reverte. His translations have earned him a number of awards, including the 2002 International IMPAC Dublin Literary Award, the 2005 *Independent* Foreign Fiction Prize, the 2008 Scott Moncrieff Prize, and the Premio Valle Inclán in 2012 and again in 2014. He is a three-time winner of the CWA International Dagger. He has spent time as translator-in-residence at the Villa Gillet in Lyons and at the Santa Maddalena Foundation.

THE EDITORS

Daniel Hahn is a writer, editor and translator (from Portuguese, Spanish and French), with forty-something books to his name. Recent books include *The Oxford Companion to Children's Literature* and translations from Brazil, Spain and Angola.

Margarita Valencia's professional life has always revolved around books, as editor, translator, literary critic, teacher. Her essays, columns and commentaries on books have appeared in – among others – *El Malpensante*, *Arcadia* and *Trama & Texturas*. She writes a monthly column for *ABC Cultural*. She has published *Palabras desencadenadas* (Unchained Words; Granada, La Veleta, 2010; Universidad de Antioquia, 2013) and *Un rebaño de elefantes* (A Herd of Elephants; Pre-textos, 2014). She currently runs the radio programme *Los libros*, which is broadcast across Colombia. She set up and since 2012 has run the Publishing Studies programme at the Instituto Caro y Cuervo.

Dear readers,

We rely on subscriptions from people like you to tell these other stories – the types of stories most publishers consider too risky to take on.

Our subscribers don't just make the books physically happen. They also help us approach booksellers, because we can demonstrate that our books already have readers and fans. And they give us the security to publish in line with our values, which are collaborative, imaginative and 'shamelessly literary'.

All of our subscribers:

- receive a first-edition copy of each of the books they subscribe to
- are thanked by name at the end of our subscriber-supported books
- receive little extras from us by way of thank you, for example: postcards created by our authors

BECOME A SUBSCRIBER, OR GIVE A SUBSCRIPTION TO A FRIEND

Visit andotherstories.org/subscribe to become part of an alternative approach to publishing.

Subscriptions are:

£20 for two books per year

£35 for four books per year

£50 for six books per year

OTHER WAYS TO GET INVOLVED

If you'd like to know about upcoming events and reading groups (our foreign-language reading groups help us choose books to publish, for example) you can:

- join the mailing list at: andotherstories.org/join-us
- follow us on Twitter: @andothertweets
- join us on Facebook: facebook.com/AndOtherStoriesBooks
- follow our blog: Ampersand

This book was made possible thanks to the support of:

Aaron McEnery · Abigail Dawson · Abigail Miller · Ada Gokay · Adam Lenson · Aileen-Elizabeth Taylor · Aino Efraimsson · Ajay Sharma · Alan Ramsey · Alana Marquis-Farncombe · Alannah Hopkin · Alasdair Thomson · Alasdair Hutchison · Alastair Maude · Alastair Laing · Alastair Gillespie · Alastair Dickson · Alec Begley · Alex Martin · Alex Ramsey · Alex Sutcliffe · Alex Gregory · Alexandra de Verseg-Roesch · Alexandra Citron · Ali Smith · Ali Conway · Alice Brett · Alice Nightingale · Alison Lock · Alison Hughes · Alison Layland · Allison Graham · Allyson Dowling · Alyse Ceirante · Amanda · Amanda DeMarco · Amanda Dalton · Amelia Ashton · Amelia Dowe · Amine Hamadache · Amy Allebone-Salt · Amy McDonnell · Andrew McCallum · Andrew McAlpine · Andrew Kerr-Jarrett · Andrew Rego · Andrew McCafferty · Andrew Marston · Andy Madeley · Angela Everitt · Angela Creed · Ann Van Dyck · Anna Solovyev · Anna Vinegrad · Anna Milsom · Anna Britten · Anna Holmwood · Anna-Maria Aurich · Annalisa Quaini · Annalise Pippard · Anne Stokes · Anne Carus · Anne Marie Meadows · Anne Marie Jackson · Annie McDermott · Anonymous · Anonymous · Anonymous · Anthony Carrick · Anthony Quinn · Antonia Lloyd-Jones · Antonio de Swift · Antony Pearce · Aoife McCarthy · Aoife Boyd · Archie Davies · Arline Dillman · Asako Serizawa · Asher Norris · Audrey Mash · Avril Joy · Barbara Devlin · Barbara Anderson · Barbara Robinson · Barbara Mellor · Barbara Adair · Barry Hall · Barry John Fletcher · Bartolomiej Tyszka · Belinda Farrell · Ben Schofield · Ben Thornton ·

Benjamin Morris · Benjamin Judge · Bernard Devaney · Beth Mcintosh · Bianca Winter · Bianca Jackson · Bill Myers · Blanka Stoltz · Bob Richmond-Watson · Brendan McIntyre · Briallen Hopper · Brigita Ptackova · Bruno Angelucci · China Mieville · Candida Lacey · Carl Emery · Carla Coppola · Carol McKay · Carole Hogan · Caroline Smith · Caroline Maldonado · Caroline Perry · Cassidy Hughes · Catherine Taylor · Catrin Ashton · Cecilia Rossi and Iain Robinson · Cecily Maude · Charles Lambert · Charlotte Holtam · Charlotte Whittle · Charlotte Ryland · Charlotte Murrie & Stephen Charles · Chris Holmes · Chris Vardy · Chris Wood · Chris Stevenson · Chris Lintott · Chris Watson · Chris Day · Chris Gribble · Chris Elcock · Christine Carlisle · Christine Luker · Christopher Jackson · Christopher Terry · Christopher Allen · Ciara Ní Riain · Claire Trevien · Claire Williams · Claire C Riley · Clarissa Botsford · Clifford Posner · Clive Bellingham · Clodie Vasli · Colin Burrow · Colin Matthews · Courtney Lilly · Dan Pope · Daniel Rice · Daniel Arnold · Daniel Venn · Daniel Coxon · Daniel Gallimore · Daniel Gillespie · Daniel Lipscombe · Daniel Gallimore · Daniel Carpenter · Daniel Barley · Daniel Hahn · Daniela Steierberg · Dave Young · Dave Lander · Davi Rocha · David Johnstone · David Shriver · David Smith · David Higgins · David Johnson-Davies · David Hedges · David Roberts · David Hebblethwaite · Dawn Hart · Debbie Pinfold · Deborah Jacob · Deborah Bygrave · Denis Stillewagt and Anca Fronescu · Dermot McAleese · Dianna

Campbell · Dimitris Melicertes · Dominique Brocard · Duncan Ranslem · Duncan Marks · Ed Tallent · Elaine Rassaby · Eleanor Maier · Elisabeth Jaquette · Eliza O'Toole · Elizabeth Heighway · Elizabeth Cochrane · Elsbeth Julie Watering · Emily Williams · Emily Gray · Emily Diamand · Emily Taylor · Emily Jeremiah · Emily Yaewon Lee & Gregory Limpens · Emma Turesson · Emma Perry · Emma Bielecki · Emma Timpany · Emma Teale · Emma Yearwood · Emma Louise Grove · Erin Louttit · Eva Tobler-Zumstein · Ewan Tant · Fawzia Kane · Finbarr Farragher · Fiona Marquis · Fiona Malby · Fiona Graham · Fiona Quinn · Fran Sanderson · Frances Hazelton · Francis Taylor · Francisco Vilhena · Friederike Knabe · Geoff Thrower · Gabrielle Turner · Gabrielle Crockatt · Gavin Collins · Gawain Espley · Genevra Richardson · Genia Ogrenchuk · Geoffrey Urland · George Wilkinson · George Savona · George McCaig · George Quentin Baker · George Sandison & Daniela Laterza · Georgia Mill · Georgia Panteli · Gerard Mehigan · Gill Ord · Gill Boag-Munroe · Gillian Spencer · Gillian Stern · Gina Dark · Glenys Vaughan · Gordon Cameron · Graham & Steph Parslow · Graham R Foster · Gregory Conti · Guy Haslam · Hannah Jones · Hannah Perrett · Hans Lazda · Harriet Mossop · Harriet Owles · Heather Fielding · Helen Jones · Helen Asquith · Helen Poulsen · Helen Weir · Helen Collins · Helen Brady · Helene Walters-Steinberg · Henriette Heise · Henrike Laehnemann · Henry Hitchings · Ian Holding · Ian Stephen · Ian Kirkwood · Ian Barnett · Ian McMillan · Ignês Sodré · Ingrid Olsen · Inna Carson

· Irene Mansfield · Isabella Weibrecht · Isobel Dixon · Isobel Staniland · J Collins · Jack McNamara · Jack Brown · Jacqueline Haskell · Jacqueline Crooks · Jacqueline Taylor · Jacqueline Lademann · Jakob Hammarskjöld · James Kinsley · James Attlee · James Warner · James Beck · James Tierney · James Scudamore · James Clark · James Portlock · James Cubbon · Jamie Walsh · Jan Vijverberg · Jane Keeley · Jane Crookes · Jane Woollard · Jane Brandon · Jane Whiteley · Janet Mullarney · Janette Ryan · Jasmin Kate Kirkbride · Jasmine Gideon · JC Sutcliffe · Jean-Jacques Regouffre · Jeff Collins · Jeffrey Davies · Jen Hamilton-Emery · Jennifer Humbert · Jennifer Hearn · Jennifer O'Brien · Jennifer Higgins · Jennifer Hurstfield · Jenny Newton · Jeremy Faulk · Jeremy Weinstock · Jess Conway · Jess Howard-Armitage · Jess Parsons · Jessica Hopkins · Jethro Soutar · Jim Boucherat · Jo Harding · Joanna Luloff · Joanna Flower · Joel Love · Johan Forsell · Johanna Eliasson · Johannes Menzel · Johannes Georg Zipp · John Hodgson · John Griffiths · John Kelly · John Down · John Royley · John Steigerwald · John Conway · John Gent · Jon Riches · Jon Lindsay Miles · Jonathan Watkiss · Jonathan Evans · Jonathan Ruppin · Joseph Schreiber · Joseph Cooney · Joshua Gray · Joshua Davis · JP Sanders · Judith Blair · Julia Rochester · Julia Thum · Julian Lomas · Julian Duplain · Julie Van Pelt · Julie Gibson · Juliet Swann · Kaarina Hollo · Kapka Kassabova · Katarina Trodden · Kate Beswick · Kate Cooper · Kate Gardner · Kate Pullinger · Kate Griffin · Katharina Liehr · Katharine Freeman · Katharine Robbins · Katherine Green ·

Katherine Sotejeff-Wilson · Katherine Skala · Katherine El-Salahi · Kathryn Edwards · Kathryn Bogdanowitsch-Johnston · Kathryn Lewis · Katie Brown · Katja Bell · Keith Dunnett · Keith Walker · Kelly Russell · Kent McKernan · Kevin Winter · Kevin Brockmeier · Kiera Vaclavik · KL Ee · Kristin Djuve · Krystalli Glyniadakis · Lana Selby · Lander Hawes · Lara Touitou · Laura Willett · Laura Batatota · Laura Drew · Lauren Ellemore · Lauren McCormick · Laurence Laluyaux · Leanne Bass · Leeanne O'Neill · Leigh Vorhies · Leonie Schwab · Lesley Watters · Lesley Lawn · Leslie Rose · Linda Dalziel · Linda Broadbent · Lindsay Brammer · Lindsey Stuart · Lindsey Ford · Linette Bruno · Liz Wilding · Liz Ketch · Liz Clifford · Lizzie Broadbent · Loretta Platts · Lorna Bleach · Louise Bongiovanni · Luc Verstraete · Lucia Rotheray · Lucy Webster · Lucy Caldwell · Luke Healey · Luke Williams · Lynn Martin · M Manfre · Mac York · Maeve Lambe · Maggie Redway · Maggie Livesey · Maggie Humm · Maggie Peel · Maisie & Nick Carter · Mandy Boles · Margaret Irish · Margaret Jull Costa · Margaret E Briggs · Maria Cotera · Marie Bagley · Marina Castledine · Mark Waters · Mark Lumley · Mark Ainsbury · Marlene Adkins · Martha Gifford · Martha Nicholson · Martin Brampton · Martin Conneely · Martin Price · Mary Wang · Mary Nash · Mathias Enard · Matt & Owen Davies · Matthew Smith · Matthew O'Dwyer · Matthew Geden · Matthew Thomas · Matthew Francis · Maureen McDermott · Maxime Dargaud-Fons · Meaghan Delahunt · Megan Wittling · Melissa Beck · Melissa Quignon-Finch · Melvin Davis · Merima Jahic · Meryl Hicks ·

Michael Ward · Michael Aguilar · Michael Moran · Michael Holtmann · Michael Johnston · Michelle Bailat-Jones · Michelle Roberts · Michelle Dyrness · Milo Waterfield · Miranda Persaud · Miranda Petruska · Mitchell Albert · Monika Olsen · Morgan Lyons · Murali Menon · Najiba · Naomi Kruger · Nasser Hashmi · Natalie Smith · Natalie Steer · Nathan Rostron · Nayla Hadchiti · Neil Griffiths · Nell Pretty · Nia Emlyn-Jones · Nick Rombes · Nick Sidwell · Nick Chapman · Nick James · Nick Nelson & Rachel Eley · Nicola Hart · Nina Alexandersen · Nina Power · Nuala Watt · Octavia Kingsley · Olga Zilberbourg · Olivia Payne · Olivia Heal · Olivier Pynn · Owen Booth · Pamela Ritchie · Pat Morgan · Pat Crowe · Patricia McCarthy · Patricia Appleyard · Patrick Owen · Paul Griffiths · Paul Munday · Paul Bailey · Paul Brand · Paul Jones · Paul Gamble · Paul Hannon · Paul Myatt · Paul C Daw · Paul M. Cray · Paula Ely · Paula Edwards · Penelope Hewett Brown · Peter Vilbig · Peter McCambridge · Peter Vos · Peter Rowland · Philbert Xavier · Philip Warren · Philippa Wentzel · Phillip Canning · Phyllis Reeve · Piet Van Bockstal · PJ Abbott · PM Goodman · Poppy Collinson · PRAH Recordings · Rachael MacFarlane · Rachael Williams · Rachel Carter · Rachel Lasserson · Rachel Kennedy · Rachel Van Riel · Rachel Watkins · Rea Cris · Read MAW Books · Rebecca Braun · Rebecca Carter · Rebecca Rosenthal · Rebecca Moss · Réjane Collard-Walker · Rhiannon Armstrong · Richard Priest · Richard Steward · Richard Ross · Richard Gwyn · Richard Major · Richard Ellis · Richard Soundy · Richard Dew · Richard Martin · Richard Jackson · Richard Hoey &

Current & Upcoming Books